RED SINAI

24 HOUR THRILLER

JOSEPH MATHERS

A division of Red Jackal Books Ltd
24 Mid Shore Pittenweem, KY10 2NL

This book is a work of fiction. Any references to historical events, real people, or real places are used fictitiously. Other names, characters, places and events are products of the author's imagination and any resemblance to actual events or places or persons, living or dead, is entirely coincidental.

For more information about special discounts for bulk purchases, please contact
Red Jackal Books Sales at +44 07513367322.

The Red Jackal Books team can bring authors to your live event. For more information or to book an event, visit our website at redjackalbooks.co.uk

Designed by David Prendergast

Manufactured in the United Kingdom

ISBN 978-1-7392781-2-0

To my family without whose love and support
this book wouldn't have been possible

Prologue

The wires spread out like a giant spider pinned to the wall, its legs criss-crossing in every direction. Freya was terrified as she fumbled and struggled with its tentacles.

Shit, there's too many.

She breathed deeply, steadying her racing heart. She was not an explosives expert, but she continued, knowing how many lives were at stake. It was extremely fragile, the cords connecting the receiver to the main central container were frayed and had clearly been soldered in a hurry. She also couldn't identify the power source, it seemed to be connected to a battery somehow but she couldn't locate it. She took another deep breath and focused on finding the initiator.

There isn't time.

She followed the wires with her fingers and guessed that it was probably inside the black central container. She carefully placed her screwdriver into the rivet on the top right hand corner screw of the lid, turning very slowly. She breathed deeply and waited, then kept turning, feeling a slight resistance in the webbing. Suddenly a switch slammed back, it clunked with a bracing metallic sound. The whole device shuddered, the spasm started in the middle and moved outwards like a shockwave. Petrified, she imagined fire exploding upwards from the ordinance and consuming her. Steadying a surge of adrenalin, she paused, took a moment to wipe away some sweat and tried to relax her shoulders.

Focus

Letting her mind go blank again, she removed the lid and carefully placed it on the floor. She repositioned her torch in her mouth and used both hands to investigate the threads trying to find the initiator. They were tangled and in some places she couldn't tell which were connected to which. She loosened several clumps of wires with her hands and attempted to get her multi tool in underneath the main bunch. Finally, she found it, buried inside an inner black box connected to the main charge with a few multi-coloured strands. She put it aside for one moment and turned back to the rest of the IED, thinking about how to defuse it. Reaching into the tool bag she grabbed an ammeter and separated the wires into different chunks, methodically testing the power levels of each one and very carefully not disturbing the rest of the device.

Slowly.

She tried loosening the lid of the central black box containing the initiator, gradually feeling each wire to check for any give in them. She had to separate the initiator from the receiver somehow. She grabbed her torch checking the destination of a group of red wires, when something went wrong. Bright green lights erupted internally and the receiver turned on.

23 Hours Earlier

PART 1

Crisis

7:00 to 8:00 AM

London

It was deathly cold at 7 am in London; the streets were deserted as few ventured out into the constant wind. The small motorcade of armoured Jaguars met little resistance as they traversed the roads on their way to Downing Street. Passing through Lambeth, the convoy picked up speed and erupted on to the heavily lit approach towards Westminster Bridge.

The beams of streetlights fell across the road producing dark shadows that ensnared the collection of vehicles. At the junction, floating pieces of ice meandered across the Thames and a flutter of pigeons managed to find some shelter from the wind on the east side of the road.

Faisal Jarvis, the UK Foreign Secretary, sat in the back seat of the middle vehicle reviewing Eastern NATO defence updates. He wanted to be up to speed when he walked into his first plenary session at the NATO defence summit taking place that morning. He was a studious man, conservative, old fashioned and likable. He worked hard for his family, his country, a man made of coarse material. He believed firmly that life was about duty and sacrifice. A former paratrooper, his deepest values were firmly rooted in his upbringing. He was not popular for his charm or humour but deeply respected by all those who knew him intimately.

In the front seat was Brian Jones, a former SAS man from Wales, a hulking figure who grew up on a farm. He won a medal for bravery in Afghanistan; when under fire he had engaged two insurgents, jumped over a wall and rescued an injured comrade. Despite receiving a lot of stick for being Welsh his troopers loved him. His eyes flickered around the immediate vicinity of the car, hyper aware of any impending danger. To his right, was Thomas Macreal, father of two small children and one of the Ministerial drivers. He was of average intelligence but reliable and less well known to the other two men. They passed the intersection and then, without warning, the ignition of the car petered out and the lead vehicle stopped abruptly. Thomas was forced to slam on the brakes.

Faisal looked up from his briefing notes, taken completely by surprise. What sounded like a car backfiring at first, suddenly exploded in a cacophony of noise encompassing the whole vehicle. Brian yelled, "Get down."

Faisal undid his seatbelt and dropped down into the footwell as the bullets rocked the car from side to side.

Brian yelled at Thomas, "Drive. Go."

Thomas yelled back and hit the dashboard. "It's dead."

Faisal covered his head with his hands, hot molten panic filled his stomach; he felt sick, a torrent of adrenalin rushing into his system. His hair stood on end and he began to hyperventilate. As the back window shattered, he shook his hair to dispel the pieces of glass falling in all directions.

"Stay down. Sir. Stay down." Brian screamed. Thomas was frantically turning the ignition, trying to get the car moving.

Now Brian was on the radio, pleading desperately for backup. Faisal looked for the other firearms officers but couldn't see them, they must also be pinned down in their cars. He forced himself to breathe slowly, remembering his military training and the time he had been under fire before. More rounds impacted the car from all directions. He hugged himself tighter, praying for the terrifying projectiles to stop.

Think. Faisal didn't know what to do. Should I run? The whirring noise increased as Thomas fought with the car. Another passenger window shattered onto the back seat.

Brian shouted, "Stay down sir. They can't penetrate the metal. Stay down."

Faisal was desperate, "Why aren't we moving?" he shouted while shaking the glass from his hair again.

Brian was on the radio again crying out for help. He yelled again at Thomas, "Get us out of here."

Thomas looked round and shook his head.

Brian noticed that the lights had gone off on the dashboard and said, "Fuck." He hit the dashboard hard. "Fuck, fuck." He looked to the left and withdrew his side arm.

He was sad, he thought of the faces of his wife and children. I can't die here; I must not die here. He desperately wanted to see his children grow up. He clenched his fists tightly as more shots continued to hiss, destroying the outer exterior of the Jaguar.

"I'm going to get you out of here." Brian turned around, "Help's coming sir."

He turned back to the dashboard forcing the control panel open. He was grappling with a cluster of wires. The side door was beginning to cave in from the impact of repeated waves of gunfire. Brian began disentangling a set of connectors, trying to get the ignition started again.

"Stay down, Sir." He yelled again.

Faisal said to Brian, "Where the fuck are they?"

"Coming."

The bullets suddenly ceased and his heart leapt. There was silence, nothing moved, the air hung with an unbearable tension. He poked his head up slowly; Brian had stopped talking, his M4 Carbine drawn. Faisal dropped his head again and listened intently for any noise.

He heard a helicopter far away, some sirens in the distance and nothing else. His security officer left the car, pistol drawn, using the door as cover. He fired two rounds but was then hit with a wave of automatic fire that shattered the window. Thomas tried to flee from the driver's door and was immediately shot in the back.

The passenger window smashed, Faisal covered his face and then nothing more.

7:12

Freya

Just five miles away, Freya Caroline Mathews was eating breakfast and reading the newspaper. She was enjoying the moment's pause preceding her workday and was carefully stirring her cornflakes. Freya was thirty-five and her face was bright, radiating with intensity. Her golden hair and clear blue eyes both betrayed her Scandinavian roots, slender and fit, years of military training had kept her in excellent shape and she had a brutal daily exercise regime.

As the sun rose higher, light streamed in through the window and her mother began to wake. She clattered about the landing and then started to hobble down the stairs. Freya immediately abandoned her cornflakes and came forward to assist her with each step. She had pleaded with her mother many times to change the arrangement of the house so that she didn't need to keep going up and downstairs but she had refused. It pained her to see Jane this way, each day finding every step more and more difficult. Eventually she sat her down on her normal chair and began to get out her breakfast. It was the same every day, one boiled egg and brown bread soldiers.

"Freya, you don't have to do this for me, love."

"Yes, I do." She said kindly.

She continued getting everything out for her and making her feel settled, but she could tell that something was wrong. She looked at her and Jane glanced towards her printed end of year evaluation on the table.

"Everything OK?" Freya said and her mother didn't respond. "You read it, didn't you?"

"Sorry, love. I... I just worry about you."

"Mum, if you want to know about anything you can just..."

"I know, but they said some things. Are you worried?"

Freya smiled and laughed, "No."

"But they said you upset people and you are ruthless in..."

"Don't worry about that, Mum, it's just office politics." She added, "My boss is an asshole."

"Freya, you shouldn't say that."

"Look, Mum, they get upset with me because I don't play by their rules. But I'm the best at what I do. Trust me, there's no need to worry."

"But I do worry, love. Your job, you know that's all you've got."

"I have you."

"But I'm old, Freya. You need something else..." she paused.

Freya rolled her eyes. Here we go again.

"Mum, I'm happy."

"I know you think that, love, but everyone needs someone."

Freya was starting to get angry and wanted to close down the conversation.

"Mum, I don't want or need a boyfriend."

"But you are…"

"Now eat your breakfast."

It was a recurring conversation; it had made Freya livid at first but after some time she had realised that it was just that her mother cared for her. So deeply that even though it made Freya angry she kept bringing it up, hoping that it might make her happy one day. She also didn't much care for her end of year report. She actually enjoyed smashing heads together, shaking things up, no matter who she upset in the process. If she had to bulldoze the opposition to get things done then so be it. Those men in cigar smoke-filled rooms could say what they liked about her. She knew this attitude had curtailed her rise through the ranks but Freya couldn't care less. She didn't want to spend more time shuffling paper; sitting behind a desk was boring and managing other people's emotions was exhausting. Her passion was getting the bad guys and more management meant more time letting others do the fun stuff.

As the sun rose higher across the horizon, long shadows rippled across the courtyard shining off the ice hidden in every crack. Their home was an attractive property in a backstreet of Walworth. The kind of place that only a few young professionals in London could afford. Freya struggled financially before she started looking after her mother and she had lived in a much more modest flat far away from the more sought-after parts of London. Her home had started life as a Georgian terrace and was sandwiched between the two other houses in either direction. It looked out of place given its relative size to the others but for Freya this was part of its appeal. It was quirky and had character, not your run of the mill property. She loved the way its quaint chimney pots jutted up into the sky.

The rear of the house was partly original but the back had been expanded much later into the garden with a dining room extension. It spread out haphazardly snaking into a small kitchen garden where they had planted some vegetables. The modifications were not in keeping with the rest of the house. But it provided extra living space that Freya appreciated. There was one major drawback however. The back wall was coated in climbing ivy which ensnared the outer fringes of the house. In the centre of this wall stood a reinforced wooden garden door which connected to a passage that ran the length of all the houses in the row. It was locked at both ends during the night but remained a security concern. It was a niggle for Freya but she loved the house so much that she had decided to put up with it. But she knew that any experienced special ops team would have loved this entry point. It provided visibility cover and an easy way to approach the house in the dark without being seen. For this reason, Freya had installed a reinforced steel wooden panelled door and added several security devices along its route so she could monitor anyone toing and froing down the winding path.

She began packing up her bag hurriedly, knowing that she was already late, and slung her things over her shoulder. She rushed into the kitchen to say goodbye to Jane. She spoke before Freya had a chance to, "Goodbye, love". She paused and in between the hug said, "Have a good day."

"Call me if you need anything," Freya replied.

"Yes, love."

She made her way out into the cold, wrapping her scarf more tightly against her face. As she stepped into the road, the shadows of the early morning sunshine spread across the tarmac and a batch of leaves gently blew across the pavement. Her encrypted MI5-issued phone buzzed, there was a red flashing box saying priority one.

Oh shit, something very serious must have happened; she hoped intensely that they hadn't been hit again. She began to half walk half run, rushing to get to work, avoiding some icy puddles as she moved, skipping from side to side.

30 seconds later she received a call.

"Freya." It was the duty officer. "The whole section has been red flashed."

"Please tell me something I don't know."

He seemed taken aback.

"Come on, man. Do you know why?"

"No."

"Well, call me back when you do."

A red flash meant a top tier national security emergency. This was only her second experience of one; the last was seared into her memory. On 7/7 several improvised explosive devices had annihilated two buses and six tube carriages. Freya remembered the ripped and bloody clothes, unidentifiable body parts scattered across the road, the rancid smell of burning human flesh. Children wandering around aimlessly surrounded by falling dust - she vowed then that she would not let it happen again. Not on her watch. Not now, not ever, not in her city.

In the distance she could hear two police helicopters in the sky, their dull drone stuck out amongst the background noise. She checked her phone again, no news yet. She walked into Thames House, the headquarters of MI5, and placed her personal effects into the grey plastic tray. They were scanned intently by a millimetre wave detector and a backscatter X-ray. She then locked her personal phone in her locker and continued through the security screen.

She asked Omar, the security officer, "Do you know what's happened?"

He shook his head. Entering the central atrium, she paid homage to the pictures of the great leaders of MI5 that lined the wall. As she passed through the door at the end of the corridor, Simon came rushing towards her. Before she could utter a sound he said, "Freya wehavean emergency". He ran the words so quickly that she barely got hold of them, but she responded very clearly and slowly.

"Simon, slow down, tell me, what happened?"

"The Foreign Sec's car was attacked."

"Shit," she shouted, "any reports of casualties? Is the area sealed off?"

"Yes, the Metropolitan police are currently sealing off the area as we speak." He continued, "Not sure about casualties."

"How many gunmen? What were they armed with?"

"Unclear and I don't know."

"OK. Briefing in 15 minutes. Get the team in now."

7:34

Prime Minister James

In Downing Street, the prime minister sat at his desk in the cabinet office reading the morning's papers. A daily ritual, it was one of the few moments in his schedule that he could be alone before the mass onslaught of officials, cabinet ministers and MPs began. Around him, his workspace represented his priorities, everything superfluous to his ambitions was jettisoned. It contained little of the clutter of previous prime ministers. Above to his left his great hero Margaret Thatcher presided over him, her portrait catching the glow of the desktop lamp illuminating his paper. On the desk to the right there was a framed photograph of his son Luke. This was given pride of place on the table and every other object seemed to be mirrored towards it. He had been tragically killed by a roadside bomb in Iraq, the PM had never recovered from the loss and he still lost his composure whenever anyone mentioned it. Friends noticed that following this tragic episode, the core of his character shifted; his comedic and sunny disposition had been replaced by something more ruthless and calculating.

He was a balding man, well past his prime. The dome-like shape of his head and physical appearance did not give him the charisma to lead a country. Neither did his greying half beard or developing tummy. It was his power of oratory, his ability to inspire others with his words and bring them into his vision. But those times had gone - the years had ground him down. Now he was a shell of a man kept alive by toughness and mental fortitude. As he continued reading the morning papers, a smile started to develop across his face, enlarging the contours of his cheeks. He was pleased that his government was receiving some positive coverage for a change. There was a great two-page spread in The Times about their hosting of the grand NATO summit and they had described his Chatham House speech about the future of Britain as "inspirational".

Then he had heard the news.

Frank Hill the Cabinet Secretary had burst in and told him in a panicky voice that Faisal's car had been attacked. They had immediately turned on the news for updates and saw that nothing was breaking yet. Another five minutes passed and Hill hung up his phone to say that the MET had confirmed Faisal's death.

Instantly the cabinet office had become noisy and chaotic. His schedule had been cleared and the room was filled with intelligence analysts, military chiefs, civil servant advisors and political leadership. Some joined by video as they hadn't arrived at work yet. He sat down at the cabinet table surrounded by them all. As the meeting started the room became quiet.

The Prime Minister began angrily, "OK, I want to know. Who did this?"

Sir Charles Chambers, the head of MI5, was the first to speak and he leaned forward slightly as he did so. He was a civil servant through and through. Traditional, career orientated, obsessive and holding a deep conviction concerning the power of government to preserve tradition. He was not charismatic, but he was a ruthless administrator who had a handle on the plethora of different agencies that made up the sprawling mass of MI5. By happy accident he had been attending an early morning working breakfast in another part of Whitehall and was able to attend the meeting this early in person.

He started, "We don't know sir. The NSC, the MET counter terror, MI6 and MI5 have all drawn blanks."

He brushed back his brown hair and continued, "But it must be someone with considerable resources and knowledge of our security protocols. Can I recommend, Sir, that we take all national security tier one targets to a secure location and we implement Horus?"

The Prime Minister nodded and a senior aide strode out of the room to make the arrangements. Horus was a code word meaning that they had a breach in security and a serious national emergency affecting all tier 1 officials. Now there would be a complete swathe of changes, a secure lockdown of all government buildings, stepped up patrols, personnel changes, security code switches and an investigation into the security breach.

He looked at each of them in turn. "There will be time to grieve for Faisal."

He added gravely, "But that time is not now."

He paused, "Right now, we must do everything we can to counter serious loss of life."

No one replied, everyone was still in shock. He turned to the attending aides and gave orders. "I want extra security to all transport terminals and areas of national security interest. Cancel police and military leave."

The government personnel looked at the Prime Minister in shock, surprised by his assertiveness. For weeks now his premiership had been on the rocks, a slight shift in the tide could have seen him replaced by a number of challengers. But this crisis had immediately stirred something deep inside him. There was a new fire in his eyes and an energy to his instructions. Pencils began scribbling frantically to keep pace with the torrent of instructions.

It continued unabated until, "Get 23SAS down here from Hereford and we need additional security for all public officials."

The room became alive with activity as civil servants scuttled across the carpet, making phone calls and busying themselves to comply with the instructions. The resources of the state were being marshalled. A man hunt had begun, perhaps the biggest the country had ever experienced. In the newspaper offices nearby, journalists were now breaking the news to the public. There were rumours circling everywhere and few hard facts. Blog posts began to appear with nothing other than personal conjecture. In Downing Street, the Prime Minister pulled his Home Secretary to one side.

Laura Williams was perhaps the Prime Minister's least favourite minister. He had given her the Home Office brief hoping it would clip her wings a bit, keeping her so busy with a huge sprawling department that it would prevent her from plotting. Unfortunately, the opposite had been true, she had confronted the challenge head on and used the platform to elevate her standing within the party and gain name recognition throughout the country. He knew that she desperately wanted to be Prime Minister and would stab him in the back at the first opportunity. Despite this he needed her, she oversaw a significant faction of MPs who were crucial to governing effectively.

"Did we have anything on this?"

His Home Secretary replied, "There was nothing, no chatter."

The Prime Minister was relieved. For a brief window party politics had been put to one side as they all dealt with the immediate crisis.

"Someone is sending us a message." He paused and then enquired, "Could this be the Russians or Chinese?"

The Chairman of the National Security Council Martin was clearly concerned but not jumping to conclusions. "It would be a serious escalation, Sir, but we can't rule it out." He continued, "Nothing has come up during routine security sweeps, no extra Chinese or Russian activity or nationals recently."

"Do you think they are trying to kill the agreement?"

He shook his head. "I don't know."

"Do you think they might strike again?"

Again he shook his head.

The Prime Minister became frustrated. "God damn it. What can you tell me!!"

They looked at each other, unsure what to say, used to the Prime Minister's frequent outbursts but still taken aback. "What about your assets in the embassy?" The PM said desperately, calming down a little.

Again they shook their heads.

He nodded and continued, in a forceful tone. "We need to find out who did this immediately," he shouted, clenching his fist and slamming the table.

He was clearly livid and neither of the officials replied, they were confused. The machinery of government and cabinet thought they had the measure of the man. For Laura he was supposed to be among the list of forgettable prime ministers, kept in power by their lack of bright ideas and ability to avoid splitting the membership. But as he looked left and right, sitting behind his desk twitching with fresh vigour, she could see that she had been desperately wrong. This worried her immensely; she had been sure that her coronation was only weeks away.

"Sarah," the PM barked, "we need a press statement in 30 minutes."

She nodded; he continued, "Have the families been informed?"

"As we speak, Prime Minister." She replied.

"They deserve our highest honour. Do you understand?" He paused, "The families must be taken care of." He demanded, then said softly, "and I want to call Faisal's wife. She needs to hear it from me."

"Understood, Prime Minister."

7:42

Trident41

Trident was in his living room. To his right perching on the table was a carefully folded newspaper and a coffee cup next to his favourite seat. Circled around his perch were wall to ceiling bookcases filled with classic volumes. He closed down his custom-made ACER AC10 Laptop barely believing what he was reading and horrified that he had been part of it. Trident struggled to stay calm, his hands trembling, his eyes darting nervously to the phone again and back, terrified to pick it up. There was a terrible battle erupting in his mind, it was requiring physical effort to call the number he knew he had to. He reached forward for the phone and then recoiled, shook his head again, angry at his own indiscipline. He rose again, this time grasping the phone and entered the number slowly with shaking hands.

They answered sharply and abruptly.

"Designator."

"Alpha Delta 493843"

The call rang for a few moments and then connected with the other party.

"Trident, why are you calling this number? It's for emergencies only."

"Did you sanction the hit on the Foreign Sec's car this morning?"

"No."

He added very quietly and slowly, "Are you saying they've gone off piste?"

He was sweating profusely now and wiped his brow with a handkerchief, he had never wanted to be part of anything like this. He clutched the phone tightly in nervousness, his hand growing white.

"No, the plan is still on track."

"I gave you Brick Fish for a different purpose..."

"Trident, you are looking at this all the wrong way; this is an opportunity."

"Jericho, we need to bring Isaiah in."

"No, we proceed as planned."

"You didn't tell me, when you contacted me…." He was struggling to keep hold of the phone now, his hands shaking erratically.

"Trident, you are in now, there is no going back, just play your part when the time comes."

"But this is not what SUEZ is……you told me you wanted to limit American power… not.."

He hung up the phone. Trident stood up from his chair and began pacing, deep lines of worry spreading across his forehead.

8:00 to 9:00 AM

Freya

The briefing room was already in chaos; coffee cups and empty sandwich boxes littered the table as techs hurried to and from their terminals eating breakfast. Spindly chairs ubiquitous in offices across the world sat motionless at right angles to the rest of the furniture. In the middle of this cacophony sat Freya surrounded by the rest of the Counter Terror Section E trying to make sense of what had just happened.

Across from her sat Simon. He was thirty-seven, unmarried, the quintessential caricature of a techy, thin arms, haphazardly dressed and a skin tone that made it clear that he spent too much time inside. Despite this Freya was incredibly fond of him and their bond was strong, they trusted each other implicitly and they both knew that they could count on each other in a crisis. Unbeknownst to Freya, Simon was deeply infatuated with her. He kept these feelings to himself, terrified of what might happen if she found out.

To his right was Fatima; recruited straight out of Cambridge University she had risen to the inner core of MI5 in just a few years. She was a hyper smart, thirty-two-year-old woman and the most softly spoken of the foursome. She was modest and kind, working quietly and methodically to uncover the evidence and pursue lines of enquiry. Her Islamic background gave her insight into the lives of many of their targets and had proved to be invaluable.

At the head of the table sat Martin. Freya deeply disliked the thirty-eight-year-old former marine but tolerated him. Unfortunately, because he worked for the security services, he behaved like a wannabe James Bond. In the office he would strut around as though on a catwalk, wanting others to notice his expensive watch, tailored suit and expansive swagger. But he lacked the inner confidence to really bring off the character. His movements and mannerisms were contrived and there was a deep disconnect between his core and outward appearance. Everyone knew that his watch was fake and the bespoke suit unbranded. For Freya, his ego spoilt the finely-balanced nature of her team. She had tried to have him removed several times, but H has said that a military liaison was essential, even though she was former military herself. She knew what he was there for; it was to keep her in check and she hated it.

The centre of government was now in complete disarray, a plethora of agencies struggled to grapple with the scale of the crisis. Multiple chains of command were being activated with few knowing who was at the front or centre of the response. Officially it was MI5, the domestic intelligence service, but now the cabinet office was taking a more direct approach. Unfortunately, the hit had yet to be declared as a terrorist incident and therefore no one knew who had operational authority.

Channels of communication were being set up between the MET police and MI5. The incident had taken place in London and therefore the MET argued they should lead gold command, with a MET police officer being the decision maker for a multi-agency response. But 'H', the operational head of MI5, had protested vigorously, arguing that since this was a counter terrorism operation they should take the lead. Frantic phone calls hadn't laid the issue to rest and for now there was no gold command. Special Branch had also got involved, sending down a number of officers to Scotland Yard who were just standing outside the building unable to get security passes because of a lack of designation. Each agency planned their own response, civil servants rushed frantically around Whitehall trying to deliver coherent information to government ministers who were demanding answers. It was a mess, but for Freya none of that mattered. She didn't wait for authorisation; she would begin her investigation immediately.

"What do we know?" she began.

"Not much," Simon replied.

Freya nodded her head towards Fatima, who stood up and moved towards the screen. Beginning to speak, she pointed to a series of detailed images taken from CCTV.

"At 6:45 this morning a black SUV turned around on Westminster Bridge and parked here." She paused. "Four heavily armed men with automatic weapons stepped on to the pavement and waited for the Foreign Sec's car to pass."

She enlarged a picture of the minister's car.

"There was some kind of electronic interference which shut down the car's computer system and meant that it came to a complete stop."

Freya began to move uncomfortably in her chair. No one said anything, but they were all unnerved by this. They were used to dealing with kids or teenagers, the kind that watched Islamist videos online and then went out to make rudimentary barely functioning explosives, or radicals who decided to drive a truck into pedestrians. Intelligence services described these operations as "low calibre plots." That's what they knew, and they were the best in the world at stopping them.

This was different; electronic hacking of secure computers was complex, extremely hard to do and would require real technical expertise. This showed a level of sophistication not seen in counter terrorism for years. Furthermore, Ministerial cars were hardened against cyber-attacks and you would need inside information on their defences to interfere with their electronics. Freya also knew that with this level of resourcing and expertise it could just be the beginning of something much bigger.

She asked, "How did they know the route of the car?"

Fatima pulled up a signals analysis profile for the area using a tablet and put it on the main screen, expertly using her fingers to highlight the most important sections. GCHQ and MI5 used this tool to map out any significant electronic interactions taking place in a geographical location. It used pattern recognition and artificial intelligence to flag any suspicious activity which could then be analysed at GCHQ. It was crucial to their work and had singlehandedly prevented several plots in the last six months.

In one recent case a terrorist cell had been tracked because of their tendency to log into their email and leave draft messages for each other within the email account, without sending them. Furthermore, they thought that using a range of devices and login locations would make it difficult to track them; in fact the opposite was true. These two activities were instantly flagged by the system as unusual and suspicious behaviour. GCHQ began their monitoring and soon broke open the cell.

She shook her head and continued, "We don't know."

She zoomed in on some interaction peaks and troughs, but most of the team understood quickly that these interactions were unrelated to their attackers.

"We checked for electromagnetic signatures emanating from the convoy." She paused. "But nothing; they weren't using a tracking device."

No one said it, but they were starting from square one with absolutely no leads. Freya looked around the room, hopeful that one of her team would think of something. Nobody spoke and she leaned back against her chair in disappointment.

At this point Martin spoke, "What about chatter?"

This was intelligence speak for the normal spike in electronic communications that happened immediately prior a terrorist strike, normally clustered among extremist websites, message groups and encrypted messaging apps.

Simon shook his head. "Nothing."

"Anything else?" Freya asked Fatima.

"No." Fatima sat back down.

Freya was angry; she took this attack as a personal and professional insult.

She began, "This happened on our watch."

She looked at each of them. "We are responsible." She emphasised the word "responsible".

"Several good men are dead because of us, now it's time for all of us to do our duty and catch these bastards before they strike again." She paused. "We are the best at what we do and let's show them that." They all nodded vigorously and she could see that they were eager to begin.

Freya began forthrightly with more specific instructions. "OK, in one hour I want to know how these people entered the UK, what kind of weapons they were using, where they got that car from, how they weren't flagged by our database and the latest forensics update."

8:13

Prime Minister James

In Downing Street, the Prime Minister was in the Cabinet Office

Briefing Room. Across from him was his Special Advisor, Sarah, and Hill, the Permanent Secretary to the Cabinet Office. He had what many regarded as the most powerful position in the government, he had direct access to the Prime Minister and oversaw the Civil Service. He also sat in on every important meeting and acted as the Prime Minister's gatekeeper.

On the screen in the corner, multiple communication channels were open. The PM had just finished conversations with the London Metropolitan Police MET, National Security Council NSC and Government Communications Headquarters GCHQ. All of them concluded that this attack was different. The NSC thought it must be state-sponsored terror, the MET maintained it was organised crime and GCHQ thought it must be terrorism related. The Prime Minister hung his head; three different agencies, three completely differing opinions. No one had yet claimed responsibility. Sarah leaned over to pass a note to the Prime Minister. It read,

Civil Contingencies Committee Meeting now

He nodded back at her and brought his previous meeting to a swift conclusion. He smiled at Sarah for a moment to thank her. She was an old family friend and he had long since been criticised for putting her at the heart of government, but he didn't care. For James, some things went above politics and on the day of Luke's death she had stood by him and comforted him in a way that defied description.

Furthermore, he wasn't sure what he would do without Sarah; she always kept him on schedule and he was also deeply fond of her as a person. She could always make him laugh on the darkest days. He also liked that she didn't try to embellish her appearance. She wasn't beautiful as such, but she was disciplined, tough and had an inner force of personality that was very attractive. She had embedded herself into the fabric of Downing Street getting to know everyone and effectively managing the spider's web of interconnections that formed around any prime minister. Often when people said "Clear it with the PM" what they really meant was "Clear it with Sarah". The PM knew that when their partnership ended with his term in office, it would hurt him deeply.

The meeting finished and the Prime Minister got up from his chair and began to leave Downing Street. As he was driven to the Cabinet Office he turned his attention back to preparing for the Civil Contingencies Committee. More commonly referred to as COBRA, it met in Cabinet Office Briefing Room A. It was a completely different beast, having a much more focused makeup, and its discussions were always designated top secret. It was formed of the heads of the NSC, MI5, MI6, the MET police, Special Branch, the Home Secretary, Chief of the Defence Staff and the Emergency Services Chief. To make decisions quickly, the other agencies were excluded and so too were most of the cabinet. The Prime Minister settled into his chair and asked for the heating to be turned up slightly. The Cabinet Office had never been properly insulated and he could feel a draught wafting in through the ancient building. He began, as others joined the meeting, "OK Bill, give us an update."

Bill, the head of the MET, straightened up and without briefing notes began, "Prime Minister, only a limited set of facts."

He spoke very calmly, his upper-class accent clearly accentuated by the rhythm of his voice. He had prepared a number of slides and began to display these in turn on the screen, taking great care to explain each one before moving to the next.

"We know that there were four attackers, CCTV confirms that they entered London Bridge travelling south just a few minutes before the attack. They seem to have had excellent knowledge of our security protocols and managed to circumvent multiple layers of protection."

He showed a video of the convoy travelling in Central London. He pointed out, "Faisal's car and other escorts stopped here in the road, for what reason we're not sure. There seems to have been some kind of electronic interference shutting down the engine, but it will be some time before we know for sure."

There were concerned looks exchanged between members of the meeting. It was another sign that this was a different kind of attack, perhaps even state sponsored; it made the agency heads very anxious. In the video the Foreign Sec's car came under fire from several directions. After about 10 seconds the first window shattered, another minute passed and a number of figures wearing balaclavas approached the vehicle.

"From the video we can make an educated guess that they used the M4A1 rifle, but this is being confirmed by Metropolitan Ballistics as we speak." He nodded towards the commander of the MET.

The video continued as more windows broke and then he paused it. Everyone knew that out of respect for Faisal he had chosen not to finish the video. He sat down without adding more detail and there was an awkward silence.

The prime minister broke the tension and pointed at the screen. "I want to know who did this and I want them apprehended TODAY," he barked "Is that understood?"

There was a murmuring of agreement around the circle. He added as an afterthought, "We need the army in on this."

There were looks across the room and several members of COBRA moved uneasily in their chairs. The chief of the defence staff spoke first. "Prime Minister, there has long been the convention that military forces should remain within their bases rather than out on the streets."

He waved that concern away.

"I know that, Michael, and I appreciate it. But I believe that the seriousness of the situation demands an upscaled response. We need to reassure the public. The military can take on routine security patrols while the MET find out who did this."

He turned to the Home Secretary, "Laura, I want you to collaborate with Michael and Bill. You turn over every stone, knock on every door, call in every asset, until we find these bastards."

She was nodding. "Bill, GCHQ can provide the specialist support, while the MET take on the investigation and, Michael, we need the military at every place of vulnerability in London."

There was clearly some unease around the table at the military being deployed to every POV but no one challenged the prime minister. Especially not during a national crisis.

The chief of the defence staff now interjected, "Prime Minister, we also need to speak about your security arrangements."

He replied curtly, "I'm fine, Michael."

"Sir," he emphasised, "It's only prudent given today's events." James nodded unwillingly.

He signalled to the others that the meeting was over and the attending senior officials got up from their chairs, rushing to carry out the Prime Minister's instructions.

8:28

Isaiah

The room was light and airy; against the back wall a cache of different weapons was propped up carefully against the skirting board. Grotesque flaps of plaster were hanging down from the ceiling and the damp spread out in all directions from the top corner of the wall. In the centre of this, a group of men sat preparing their weapons. They cleaned and oiled them like painters putting the final touches to a work of art.

Isaiah stood in the centre of the circle, he was a compact, clear-cut man, with sharp eyebrows, a lot of very soft black hair and thoughtful dark brown eyes. He had a look of wariness, which would only change when he felt relaxed or happy. Right now, he had a smile of amused friendliness and pleasure, which aroused feelings of warmth, and something more, in many of his disciples. He was a leader who possessed a quality - call it charisma, passion or leadership, the word didn't matter. But it gave him an unquantifiable power to inspire people and bind them to his cause. His second in command, Daniel, sat across from him with legs folded, an automatic weapon across his lap. His frame was the opposite of Isaiah's and he looked like a teenage kid whose features had never fully transitioned into adulthood. But, like Isaiah, there was steel in his eyes, he was smiling broadly and embraced Isaiah in a strong hug.

When they parted Daniel said, "Brother. We have plunged our first knife into their chest."

Daniel was excited about the next stage of the operation and still high on adrenalin following their successful kill. Isaiah didn't reply, he acknowledged Daniel's presence with a curt nod and moved around the room checking what the other men were doing. Daniel was dismayed that Isaiah didn't share in his immediate excitement but then he realised that his commander was simply concentrating, planning the mission ahead rather than losing his focus.

Daniel nodded, "When will the next stage begin?"

"Soon."

8:30

President Leon

The President of the United States sat in the opulent splendour of Claridge's Hotel in London, the golden interior shining as the light slowly crept up the opposite wall. He was reclining on a red and gold sofa next to a stained-glass window, which contained a beautiful sprawling mosaic of biblical scenes that reflected coloured light right across the room. He was surrounded by a few staffers, trying to read his daily national security briefing.

He was worn out. Exhausted by the excuses of the Europeans, harassed by senators wanting to have their say, buffeted by the constant turf wars amongst his staff and ground down by the final fight over this deal. But the fire burning inside of him refused to go out, he was so close to bringing about lasting change to NATO. Bringing many more states into the club, including some Middle Eastern ones. This would harden their defences against Russian and Chinese cyber aggression and make it legally binding for other NATO countries to spend 2% of their GDP on defence. It would be a spectacular success, even Regan, Clinton and the Bushes hadn't managed to pass anything like this. It would be one of the crowning achievements of his presidency.

But the British were a problem. Although gracious and well organised hosts, his relationship with the Prime Minister was frosty at best. He was a weakening nationalist and thought that Britain had been seriously damaged by its relationship with the United States. He used a sense of standing up to America to bolster his support. In the eyes of the British public and press the country had been a poodle for too long and now was the time to get tough with the great bully. Leon also knew that James blamed them for the death of his son Luke in Iraq when he was a cabinet minister. Upon meeting the Prime Minister, he could see the deep twisted knot of pain and hurt just under the surface. The President knew that he would never truly forgive them.

Unusually, the Germans had become a major ally in getting this agreement approved and there was just one more obstacle to be overcome before signing. Latvia, Lithuania and Estonia wanted all of recognised Ukraine to be part of NATO even though Crimea was currently occupied by Russia. There was resistance to this across the spectrum of NATO members because Crimea hadn't been officially recognised as part of Russia. Approving their amendment could trigger article 5 of NATO's treaty meaning that the annexation of Crimea by Russia could be seen as an act of war against all NATO members. It was a major headache, but if he could bypass this obstacle, then he could see a path towards the finish.

But the attack had changed everything; it had completely skewered their negotiations and the Secret Service were now urging him to leave immediately.

"Mr President, we should get on Marine One and go."

It was Josh, the straight-talking head of his security detail. He wouldn't normally express this in such forceful terms but it was clear that he was deeply worried. The room was in chaos; several aids were dashing across the room communicating with their teams, rescheduling meetings, drafting press statements, obtaining new information.

He smiled, "As much as I would like to, Josh, we need to finish this visit. We are so close to getting this done." He held up his fingers to show how close they were.

"I strongly advise that we go now, Sir, your security must come first. A British cabinet minister has just been assassinated one mile from here and we have no idea what might happen next."

He looked Josh directly in the eyes and said firmly, 'I'm staying."

There was no need to say any more. Josh nodded, stepped back and began talking over the radio, asking for extra security. President Leon was determined to stay and save this agreement if only to snatch some kind of recompense from all the bullshit.

8:41

Freya

In Thames House a nationwide manhunt was beginning to take shape. Assets were being called in and agent handlers had gone out to clear dead drops. A fraught series of meetings with the MET police had established gold command. A compromise had been reached; the counter terrorism branch of Scotland Yard were taking charge of the response with MI5 playing a supporting role. GCHQ was providing signals intelligence and had sent a liaison to gold command. Lines of communication were being streamlined as the state ramped up its response to the attack. Freya was sat at her desk and was contacting an old asset, seeing if he had anything on today's events.

Fatima rushed in and spoke urgently, "Freya we've got something."

She pulled out a tablet and began to show her before Freya had a chance to respond.

"One of the assailants was carrying an electronic device which was switched off. It was encrypted so we weren't able to access that much useful information. But using location metadata we were able to track some of its movements for the last 24 hours."

She showed a map on a tablet computer where a number of

electronic trails were displayed and pointed. "They remained static in one location for about 18 hours immediately prior to the attack."

"Were there any other devices close by or CCTV?" Freya's voice rose in excitement.

Fatima shook her head. "Unfortunately, they just stayed in a car park for this time and there is no footage. The MET have already been there, but nothing."

Freya was disappointed.

"But about 20 minutes before that they visited an industrial unit. Now we didn't manage to get footage of the unit but we did manage to get some footage from a CCTV camera on the slip road outside."

As Freya's heart was pounding with anticipation, Fatima methodically tapped some buttons on her tablet to open a video window.

It showed a grey drab road with concrete fringes, the same as you could find in most urban areas. They watched the attacker's car, a black SUV, drive down the road towards the industrial unit and then turn a corner to enter. The driver was driving timidly and even signalled for some time before turning left even though there was no other traffic on the road. A few minutes later a silver Lexus Es with diplomatic licence plates followed.

Freya thought, fuck, that's not good.

"Shit, which embassy is that?"

Fatima knew something and Freya realised it; she tilted her head to one side as though deciding whether to reveal the information or not. She started and then stopped, stuttering. Freya finally lost patience and folded her arms.

"Come on."

"You're not going to like it."

"Tell me."

"James Reynolds."

Freya didn't respond - she was deeply confused.

"We tracked his phone to the car and CCTV confirms his movements. He also made a call to our attackers from his car, voice recognition of the call confirms."

"But that means..."

"Yes."

"Oh shit."

9:00 to 10:00 AM

Prime Minister James

In his study, the Prime Minister sat for some time staring into space considering the implications of today's events. Just off the cabinet room, it was a sanctuary of sorts, the entrance hidden to most, the oak panelled door resembling any other room in the building. It provided a small oasis of calm in otherwise completely hectic days. An informal precedent had been set that only Sarah and Hill could disturb him here. He continued working methodically through the mass of red box papers given to him each morning. There was a knock on the door and the Prime Minister sighed.

"Enter."

Ben Cooke, the Chairman of the Joint Intelligence Committee, walked in.

"What is it, Cooke?" It was obvious something major had happened.

"MI5 and the NSC have found something, Sir."

The Prime Minister sat up in his chair, looked up from his papers and became more alert.

"They tracked an electronic device used by one of the assailants who attacked Faisal's car."

He paused and the Prime Minister didn't interrupt.

"It seems that they had a meeting 18 hours ago in which they met up with a number of other collaborators. We have evidence that the senior American military attaché was involved, sir."

The prime minister kept his face passive and said slowly, "What are you saying?"

James's advisor paused and stood motionless; he was terrified of what he was about to say next, fearing it could be career dynamite if he was wrong.

"The Americans may be aiding the terrorists."

"What?" he barked. He didn't say anything for some time, making Cooke increasingly nervous.

The PM simply replied, "No."

Cooke continued to state the intelligence service's current position, cautiously ticking off the key points with his fingers, "We are still confirming now, Sir, but we have increasing amounts of evidence. We have tracked the attaché's phone to this industrial estate at the same time as the terrorists. His movements from home match his journey through London to the target location, we have phone records of direct contact made between him and the attackers this morning, voice recognition confirms. Furthermore, we have reason to believe that the weapons given to the attackers may have been from the CIA. They match a cache that was supposedly lost some time ago, we just had confirmation from the MET ballistics team. Lastly, our security experts have told me that the cyberattack on the minister's car bears the hallmarks of a tool developed by the CIA known as Brick Fish, which they have been developing to interfere with self-driving navigation systems."

The Prime Minister's expression was unreadable; he just sat back in his chair and said nothing. Another knock on the door broke the tension; he indicated to Cooke to stay.

"What is it?" he barked, the tension now audible in his voice.

"Prime Minister, I have your daughter on the line." Sarah said.

He immediately indicated to Cooke to leave and said, "See what else you can dig up. But understand I need hard evidence on this before acting."

He nodded and left the room quickly, while the Prime Minister took the phone carried by his assistant.

He answered immediately, "Are you OK?"

"Dad, I'm confused."

He could tell by his daughter's voice that she was extremely agitated.

"What about, love?"

"They said that, they said something bad happened to Faisal"

"I'm sorry, love. Yes."

"He was so nice."

"I know."

"What happened?" Her voice sharpened.

"We don't know, love. But we're going to find out."

She was sobbing quietly.

He enquired, "Are you OK? Did you take your medication?"

"Yes, Dad."

"Probably up the dose today. Two instead of one. OK?"

"Yes, Dad."

"Freya called. Wanted to see if I was OK."

"That's good." He nodded. "She's always been a great friend to you."

"I know."

"I have to go now, but don't worry we will get this whole mess sorted out." He added as an afterthought "We're sending over some extra helpers to look after you today, they should arrive in about 15 minutes."

"Yes Dad. OK… thank you…"

"Speak soon."

The Prime Minister's solid face suddenly looked ashen and tired. He leant back and thought for a few moments, stretching his shoulders from left to right. Attempting to relieve some of the tension developing in his back, he didn't want to believe it. The timing was awful, right in the middle of the summit. But it didn't make much sense; why would they strike now? In the middle of finishing an agreement that they had spent years negotiating and executing.

But in his gut he was sure that the Intelligence Services were right. He was suddenly furious, how dare they, those fuckers. They smile at us and talk about the *special relationship*. While at the same time stabbing us in the back. After everything Britain had done for the Star Spangled Banner. After all the lives we had sacrificed in America's wars. After Luke's life was cut short, too soon, all because of those awful neo con ideologues who became obsessed with Iraq. After we had stood shoulder to shoulder with them when no one else would. It made him retch.

They would pay for this.

9:09

Freya

The meeting room was hot, the odour of body sweat began to waft through the corridors as techs rushed from meeting to meeting. Several different operations were taking place simultaneously and additional personnel were squeezed into a space not really designed for them. Half-open sandwich breakfast boxes and pieces of paper left by the drafted-in specialists were scattered about. It all added to the sense of chaos now engulfing the department.

Just outside, Freya and Fatima were sat opposite each other, heatedly debating the latest intelligence. Fatima was annoyed by Freya's intransigence; she couldn't understand her stance on the issue. As a team they tried to be rigorous and analytical with their assessment of the evidence. But for Fatima, Freya was breaking her own rules and was letting her passions control her thought process.

"It wasn't them," Freya began.

Fatima replied, "Freya, we have the ballistics, James at the same time as our attackers and an electronic trial linking them back to the CIA."

Freya didn't reply and crossed her arms.

"You just have to accept the fact that they betrayed us."

"No". Freya shook her head.

"Freya, why are you ignoring the evidence?"

"Look, Fatima, are you telling me that they were smart enough to get four guys into the middle of London under our very noses, infiltrate our government, remotely shut down a ministerial car, dodge all our layers of security, avoid leaving an electronic trail, hide themselves from CCTV?"

She breathed and then continued her speal.

"But then stupid enough to use an electronic device they know we can trace, contact the terrorists directly through a known American agent, use hacking tools we know they have been developing and give us ballistics evidence all on a silver platter - even the CIA are not that incompetent."

She sat back in her chair and acted as though the matter was settled, folding her arms

"Freya, you're not thinking clearly."

"No," she said again, not moving.

"But who else apart from the CIA have the logistics to pull something like this off? It must be state sponsored."

"It wasn't them", she said, shaking her head.

A vein throbbed in Fatima's forehead and she turned away from Freya in frustration, her face turning a deep crimson.

9:17

President Leon

The summit was continuing, although just barely. For the moment all the delegations had been locked down in their various hotels or other residencies unable to travel while the MET investigated. President Leon sat on the sofa continuing his calls with the Lithuanians, trying to offer concessions in the vain hope of trying to remove a major obstacle to this deal. Around him his staff were attempting to rally support amongst some of the other European countries to convince the Latvians and Estonians to change their stance.

Leon was in the middle of a call when his National Security Advisor walked into the room. Shane Dilalio was a straight-talking Texan and highly experienced former CIA chief who had been recently appointed to the position. He was not a policy expert but he understood how to navigate the sprawling agencies of the NSA. He was excellent at leading his staff and had a knack for choosing the right people for the right job at the right time. He always turned up to briefings with a cursory knowledge of the topic but sometimes he was unable to answer questions that required significant technical knowledge. In this situation he would often defer to more junior staffers. Unlike others, he wasn't afraid to show his lack of knowledge, which the president appreciated. As they were not due to meet for another few hours, this was a breach in protocol and he was sure it must be bad news. He tried to end the phone call with the Prime Minister of Lithuania which proved difficult. Rather than focusing on the issue at hand he had spent most of the call trying to convince him to visit. He was tired of all the politicking and just wanted them to state their final position. Rather than continuously saying maybe, he ended the call and quickly turned to his NSA.

"I'm sorry to interrupt your call, Mr President, but I have an urgent matter to discuss with you."

The President sighed and his heart fell, the tone of his voice told him everything he needed to know. Shane looked around, indicating that he didn't want the other staffers there. Leon was quick on the uptake. He said quickly, "Please give us the room."

The staffers filed out of the room, leaving just the NSA and the President facing each other. The President was now seated behind the desk and Shane stood poised in the middle of the room.

"I'm sorry to say this, Mr President, but we have a total shit storm brewing." The President nodded and appreciated the candour.

Leon paused and replied, "OK, how bad?"

"Bad, our sources within Whitehall have told us that the Intelligence Services of the United Kingdom suspect that we were instrumental in organising the attack this morning. Giving material support to the terrorists who carried out the assassination."

Hot anger filled the President's veins. "What?" He couldn't quite believe what he had just heard.

"That's ridiculous."

"I know, Sir, but it's what the British believe."

President Leon was not known for his outbursts and had been praised in many corners for how calm he was. But at this moment he wanted to scream with all the anger he could muster. The idea that the British thought that they would assassinate a senior member of their government made his blood boil. He breathed out his frustration and thought through the implications, trying to remain calm and analytical. How could he perform damage control and calm this down?

"What evidence do they have?"

"It's patchy at best. But they have an old cache of weapons apparently belonging to the CIA and they had our senior military attaché under surveillance. His movements match the terrorists the day before the attack."

"Fucking shit, fuck," Leon said under his breath trying to keep calm.

This was a disaster of epic proportions. It would torpedo this deal and could obliterate the special relationship for decades. He tried to be analytical but it was difficult. He pleaded desperately, "Shane, you've got to stop them going public with this."

He nodded and added, "Unfortunately they've already scheduled a press conference at 12."

"Do you know what it is about?"

"No, but I bet it's to announce sanctions."

"Listen to me, Shane, you move heaven and earth, you have to find out what they plan to announce in that press conference."

"Understood, Sir."

9:31

Trident41

The weather was getting worse as Trident arrived at a derelict industrial estate in the East End of London. It was freezing, the wind howled in the exposed car park and he struggled to close the door of his car. He pulled his coat tighter in a vain attempt to keep his chest warm. He was terrified and continued obsessively looking over his shoulder, paranoid that he was being followed; for the fiftieth time he touched the Glock attached to his waist. He felt very strange and was having an out of body experience. Computers were his thing, not breaking and entering.

What the hell am I doing here?

He stopped for a moment, but finally something willed him forward: the cold, fear of Suez, a sense of conviction or just sheer fright - it was hard to be sure. He continued onwards walking lopsidedly, pulled by both the fight and flight instinct.

Trident stepped inside the building nearest to the carpark moving cautiously, a broken window allowing some light to enter the space. It was airy, wide and green moss clung to its walls; columns of water fell from the holes in the ceiling. He looked over his shoulder again searching vigorously for an ambush.

Jericho stepped out of the shadows; Trident jumped backwards with fright and almost fell.

He said abruptly, "Jesus, Jericho you scared the life out of me."

Jericho didn't reply and indicated to Trident to be silent. He was dressed in a three-piece suit that was immaculate, his appearance was so unremarkable as to be noteworthy, which was intentional. To onlookers he remained a small cog in the huge government bureaucracy. His hair was even styled in such a way as to suggest this. Only his eyes gave away his true nature, the real psychopathy of a man who was ruthless and patient. His every move tailored but unconnected to any human emotion, completely choreographed by one obsession.

He looked around and said bluntly, "Were you followed?"

"No". He nodded.

Without speaking again, Trident reached into his coat and grabbed a small black box. He treated the box with great care and kept his hands very steady as he passed it to Jericho.

He nodded and said, "Let me check it."

He pulled out some kind of scanning device and stared at the view screen for a few seconds and thoroughly examined the box, being very careful not to disturb the contents.

He nodded, "Seems OK."

Trident began to walk away, wanting to escape as soon as possible. As he did so Jericho said, "One more thing."

Trident desperately wanted to leave and was half pivoting away from Jericho as he listened.

"The target has changed."

Trident didn't reply, he kept his face passive. But inside a knot of terror was squeezing his insides. He hated how the mission parameters seemed to change on a regular basis, but he was so keen on saving his skin that he didn't say anything.

"You'll receive an updated mission brief; the mission go word is COVENTRY."

Then Jericho carefully placed the cube into a special carrying case and walked towards the entrance as quickly as he could. Trident waited for a few minutes after he left and then headed back to his vehicle - his heart didn't stop pounding until he was safely within his car.

9:47

Freya

Freya stood in the office of H, the Director General of MI5. It was a magnificent mahogany room which had been the sanctuary of every head of domestic intelligence for at least the last eighty years. Much of the clutter had been removed after the previous occupant and it now felt much more spacious. Only a chair, a table, a lamp and one picture sat on the desk. Nothing about it was personal; H didn't care much for such frivolous details - like the man the room spoke to function.

Above the desk there was a dark space in the ceiling, plastered over, there must have been a chandelier once, but now flower patterns flowed out from the centre of the ceiling in every direction towards its edges. The windows were south-facing, wide and expansive. The view was gorgeous and looked out directly over the Thames. The sunlight flowed across the room but the desk itself was left in shadow. In the centre of the room Freya and H were having another heated argument. H was sitting behind his desk and Freya was standing in the middle.

"Freya, I don't want to hear it."

"You are making a……."

She was interrupted sternly by H. "We have hard proof that the Americans were involved. Our job now is to plan the response."

"We are being played; can't you see…"

"Freya, that is enough."

"I need 2 agents and 1 tech……"

He had kept his stiff upper lip until now, but H suddenly lost his temper.

"Get out of my office Freya!" He shouted, "You can't just barge in here demanding assets! Use the established proceed…"

She interrupted him. "Sir, you need to list ..."

"Out now!!" he roared.

She left seething, slamming the door as she exited; anger was coursing through her veins, spreading out from her chest to the tips of her fingers and back. Freya followed her therapist's advice and breathed several times to control the torrent of frustration now consuming her. She breathed again but lost control and like a child went into the bathroom, screamed, hit the wall hard with her arm and then fell silent. The sharp pain in her elbow and the outpouring of emotion made her feel better almost immediately. Freya stopped for a few moments gathering her thoughts. "I'm going to take these fuckers down, with or without you, H."

She would do what needed to be done.

She decided to bypass the system. I tried to get them to listen to me but they wouldn't so therefore I have no choice, there are innocent lives at stake.

Freya left the bathroom and immediately headed downstairs. She avoided a new colleague in the corridor who tried to engage her in conversation by mouthing 'late for a meeting' and after a few minutes arrived on the lower ground level 2. The white corridors reminded her of a sterile hospital, the fringes encircled by blue skirting board and an unremarkable, mass produced grey coloured floor. The dull groan of lines upon lines of servers echoed throughout the corridor. She knew she would find Simon down here and it was the perfect place to have an undisturbed conversation. She opened a door with the notice Authorised Personnel Only. Freya wasn't authorised but that didn't matter; she needed to be there.

On both sides of the room were two stacks of servers that ran parallel, emitting a tunnel of soporific groaning. She imagined that some people would find this relaxing but for her it was eerie. She noticed that the stacks had been upgraded since she was last down here and the wiring was now much neater, embedded within the black dominoes. She began searching for Simon and thought, Fuck you, H.

She found him in the right-hand corner, he had headphones on and at first he didn't respond to her presence. She indicated to him to take off his headphones, he looked surprised but complied with the instruction.

She began insistently, "Simon, I need your help."

"Sure," he replied, leaning backwards in his chair.

"Can you run a trace on this?" She handed him an IP address written down.

"Why?" He instantly became suspicious.

She looked around, "No records, OK. Off the books."

He said nervously, "I don't know about this, Freya…." He paused, "Is this sanctioned?"

"Seriously Simon, grow a pair," she exclaimed.

He gave her a 'you are going to get me into trouble' look. "Freya," he sighed.

She urged him more softly this time. "Look I think that we're being set up and this is just to check." He wasn't convinced and still sat there with folded arms. She continued, "If you get nothing, pretend it never happened."

He finally relented and snatched the number, shaking his head as he did so, methodically typing the numbers into his computer.

"Thank you."

9:51

Prime Minister James

James was just finishing up a meeting with the party chairman. As he left, Hill came in through the open door.

The PM sighed; he had hoped for a few minutes of peace before the next interruption, Hill strode to the middle of the room and said, "Prime Minister, the President will call you in a few minutes."

This made James bristle; no one had really asked him if he would take the call – everyone just assumed that he would. But now that it had already been accepted, he had to go through with it.

"Would you like me to get the team?"

The PM nodded and Hill came forward to hand him the civil service briefing notes. There was a helpful yellow sticky note reminding him to mention Leon's wife's birthday. This again annoyed him; of course he remembered. He spent another two minutes' skim reading the briefing before pausing to look up; his chief of staff and several other special advisors were getting ready to listen in on the call.

The phone began to ring.

James picked it up, still feeling annoyed that this was simply expected, and James's staff could tell that the usual pleasantries were being dispensed with as the President got right to the point.

"Understood, Mr President"

James looked increasingly annoyed as the conversation continued.

"We are more than equipped to handle this, thank you".

There was more chatter on the other end of the line.

"No, Mr President, that is not the case."

The PM started tapping the desk and the special advisor's jaws suddenly dropped.

"Don't you dare threaten us."

There was another brief exchange between both parties.

"You did, you told me."

The special advisors were ruffling their briefing notes trying to work out what to do as the conversation became increasingly acrimonious.

"You are guests in this country and..."

He interrupted.

"I'm sorry but I've heard enough."

James put down the phone; no one said anything. Everyone present was in shock at how quickly the conversation had soured.

Only Hill spoke, "That could have gone better."

His comment really annoyed James, who didn't reply, still seething with anger.

He continued, "What do you plan to do?"

9:56

Isaiah

Daniel and others had just finished a prayer circle and were now huddled around a map of Egypt. Strewn across the map, there were a number of different coloured crosses that represented the location of cells spread out across the country. Isaiah was a technologist but sometimes he needed the touch and feel of paper. For some reason, Daniel didn't know why, Isaiah would never read the bible on a screen. He guessed that there was something about holding the text in your hands that gave the words gravity, you could feel the energy of those sacred texts through your fingers, the generations who had held them before, the message they were trying to convey.

Isaiah had in front of him several phones which he was using to communicate with a whole host of different actors. It was crucial that there was synchronisation between their campaign in London and Egypt. He planned everything to the tiniest detail but fretted about what the Egyptian security services knew. Daniel was sure they didn't know much, he felt that if they did they would almost certainly be dead or in jail already. The small group of men continued to trace out lines on the map, predicting moves and counter moves. Suddenly Jude, one of their operatives, came forward with a phone, holding his hand over the receiver.

"Daniel, there's a problem."

10:00 to 11:00 AM

Prime Minister James

In Downing Street, the Prime Minister was weighing the pros and cons of the different options for responding to the current crisis. The Intelligence services had continued to update him and to James the evidence now seemed watertight. Surrounding him were the heads of MI6, MI5, GCHQ, the Head of the Armed Forces and the acting Foreign Secretary.

"Prime Minister, we have several options for a response."

Earlier in the meeting there were shocked gasps as it was revealed they had evidence that the Americans had been involved. The Head of the Armed Forces was so angry that he pounded his fist into the table with anger and muttered, "those bastards." Debate was now raging; some participants were struggling to keep their cool. Others were attempting to argue what could be judged as proportionate action under international law. Most leaders argued in favour of their own department taking the lead. The chairman of GCHQ Michael Collins argued that a cyber-attack could be an effective deterrent against future aggression. He was more hawkish than the other members present and was keen to try out some of the tools his agency had developed. The more dovish faction was led by the acting Foreign Secretary who argued for restraint until they knew more. Adding to the confusion, there were a few COBRA members who argued that an evidence threshold hadn't been reached and their case was weak. Largely these voices were drowned out by the faction wanting blood. After this initial flurry of speculation, the Prime Minister had called the meeting to order and the Head of MI6 was now outlining a number of responses the UK government could take.

Lawrence had a commanding presence; he outlined the options succinctly and professionally. "Option 1 is to do nothing and pretend that we don't know anything about their involvement."

"Absolutely not." The Prime Minister looked shocked at the suggestion; there were nods around the room, the head of the Armed Forces was shaking his head vigorously.

"Option 2 is to recall the ambassador."

"What could be their response?" replied the Acting Foreign Secretary.

"At best they would cancel any bilateral cooperation, R&D research, recall the ambassador etc." He paused, "At worst they could suspend all cooperation and expel the British diplomatic mission from Washington."

The Prime Minister didn't interrupt.

"I must add, Sir, that any option apart from option one would mean informing the media and that will put a huge amount of strain on the transatlantic alliance. Particularly during a Presidential visit and it would torpedo any hope of clinching a deal at this summit."

The Prime Minster nodded his head to show that he understood.

"OK, option 3."

"We call an emergency session of the UN security council and protest directly to the American representative at the UN. Following that there would be a vote at the UN General Assembly and Security Council."

Judging by the atmosphere in the room there wasn't much support for that idea. They all knew that they would not win a vote, which would be a huge international embarrassment for Britain. America could also veto anything they proposed in the Security Council and there was not much friendly feeling in the General Assembly either. The committee wanted action, not to wait for several weeks to follow a UN process.

He continued, "Whether we would win it or not remains to be seen."

The Prime Minister nodded and said, "OK, option 4."

"We show evidence of collusion from the Americans with the attack today and expel the American diplomatic mission from the UK."

There were gasps when this was suggested.

"Possible response?"

"They may refuse to leave and then we may need to call in the military. We could have images of American diplomats being escorted out of the country at gunpoint. They would almost certainly expel the British diplomatic mission in response and implement sanctions."

The Prime Minister nodded again; he kept listening intently.

"Option 5?"

"We prevent American ships from entering UK waters, we expel all American military personnel from the UK, implement sanctions and close the embassy."

There were protests from around the room. "No, not here."

Others said, "I will not condone this," "What the hell are you talking about?"

The Prime Minister raised his hand to silence them.

"OK."

There were garbled voices from the assorted members of COBRA. "Prime Minister, perhaps it is easier if we just…"

They started arguing amongst themselves and it quickly became heated.

"Yes, that's right. All these options cause…."

The Prime Minster stood up, leaned forward and roared slamming the table. "Faisal is dead!!"

He paused. "Our friend!!"

"Our country has been attacked and we know who did it!!" He pointed.

The committee fell silent.

"We MUST respond to this act of aggression," he said with vigour.

Suddenly red-faced, as the others fell silent, James calmed down again. "Now does anyone else have any other options?"

Cobra fell silent and each member looked around the room wondering if any would interject.

The Prime Minister waited, paused for a few moments and then said, "We go for option 5."

Again there were protests, "BUT Prime Minister."

"The damage this will do."

He silenced them again. "We WILL not be bullied." He continued, "And the only thing that bullies react to is strength."

There were ashen faces right across the table.

"Sarah, we need a press statement," he said, rising from his chair.

"But Prime Minister what about cabinet?"

"I will address this with them immediately and get the speaker of the House of Commons on the phone; we will need a vote in the House later today."

10:14

Isaiah

Isaiah and Daniel sat with their backs against the wall taking a break. The sun had risen and light streamed across the room, they smoked hashish, the clouds of vapour gradually wafting across the room.

Daniel received a message on his phone; he looked at it for 30 seconds, smiled broadly and then said to Isaiah, "We've just had confirmation from our source, they're going to announce at 12:00."

Daniel turned towards Isaiah, gauging his reaction. Isaiah sat back considering this new development, not showing any excitement.

Daniel continued, 'It's a great success. Congratulations."

Isaiah pondered. "Yes, it is", then fixed Daniel with an icy stare, "but we must not lose our FOCUS, there is still much work to do."

He emphasised the word focus and still didn't show any more excitement. Daniel couldn't understand this, he thought they should celebrate their victory. Isaiah paused, furrowing his brow. "We might need to bring the timetable forward."

Daniel was incredulous, shaking his head. "What?"

Isaiah stood there for a minute ruminating and then said, "Contact Jericho and ask him to bring everything forward a few hours. Is the asset in place?"

"Yes." Daniel was again frustrated with Isaiah's lack of enthusiasm but did as he was ordered. He paused, "She's already in possession of the package."

He nodded, "Good."

Daniel grabbed his phone and began to dial the number.

10:33

Freya

In Thames House, a task force was meeting in the conference room. Representatives of the MET had arrived as well as several foreign

Intelligence agencies. In the lower part of the building, Freya and Simon were having a heated whispered exchange, checking over their shoulders as they did so. Simon was red faced and as the conversation continued, he looked increasingly exasperated. Freya was calmer, her hair gradually being blown into her eyes at intervals as the server-cooling fans cycled the air in the room.

"Freya, I can't believe you asked me to do this. You didn't tell me I was running a trace on a Chinese intercept."

She ignored the comment and continued, "What did you get?"

"You know I could get into so much trouble for this."

"Simon."

"How did you even know they were monitoring all the American embassy's communications?"

"I just do..."

"You know that I had to go back and cover my tracks so they didn't know I had accessed the system."

"Simon…."

"You should have told me. Sometimes I just want to…."

She held up a hand, "What did you get?"

He continued shaking his head, looking increasingly anxious. He checked over his shoulder again to make sure that no one was listening, as he moved closer to the servers. As if hoping that the noise would mask his intransigence and in an even quieter voice, he pulled out a printed list of calls and numbers.

"There were 44 calls out of the embassy in the last 24 hours; most are just general chat and we have complete transcripts, nothing interesting."

Freya didn't interrupt and allowed him to continue.

"But the call intercepted by GCHQ between James Reynolds and the terrorists had something weird about it."

Freya became excited.

He paused, "This is the call that GCHQ presented to the PM. Every phone call that takes place in London has a mast reference indicating a rough geographical location for the call. The phone call that took place has the reference number of the mast nearest to the embassy."

Freya was disappointed and her face fell.

"But it seems that the call switched masts while they were speaking."

Her mood brightened, "So that means?"

He began to explain more slowly. "The embassy is in the middle of the coverage for the masts so there shouldn't be a break in coverage, which suggests that they made the call somewhere else. The GCHQ tech guys probably didn't notice because supplementary mast references are automatically deleted and calls are logged under the first mast the phone uses to make the call."

"Do you know where the conversation took place?"

"Yes."

Freya clapped her hands together. "Simon, thank you."

Simon added "Be careful, Freya. Whoever did this knew how to fool our system and also knew where the coverage areas overlap."

Freya didn't say anything to this. Too excited to reply, she hugged Simon tightly and he was temporarily speechless. Too shocked to say anything.

"Freya, take this seriously."

She didn't listen, she was smiling from ear to ear, she rushed towards the door of the server room saying as she did so, "Send it to my phone." And quickly disappeared.

He wrote, Sunderland Street, London SW11 9OT

10:47

Trident41

Back at home, Trident felt a tumour of anxiety growing within him. He didn't want to speak to them and he hated conversing over the phone. It was dangerous; any conversation could be recorded or tracked but they had called him and he was scared.

Jericho started "Are you tracking them?"

"Yes, but there's been an update, my system access is diminishing."

It was a lie; he simply didn't want to continue doing this.

He replied, "OK, I want to know exactly what response they are planning."

Trident then stayed silent for 30 seconds, sending him the relevant data.

"Jericho, what is Isaiah planning?"

"Not your concern", Jericho continued.

"When I joined SUEZ I thought you were going to slowly limit American power….."

"Trident, stop it. Just….."

"I don't want to destabilise the whole government."

"Stop this."

Jericho suddenly became uncharacteristically angry and Trident cowered. "Look, Trident, we have no choice; someone must do something. We are always clearing up the mess the Americans make of the world." He shouted and continued his rant, "Thousands of British soldiers are DEAD. Our economy is in RUINS." He said accusingly, "And what the fuck have we done about it?" He paused, breathing heavily.

Trident didn't reply.

"Today it ends. All of it."

11:00 to 12:00 AM

Prime Minister James

In the Prime Minister's private study, the heating was on full. Unfortunately, it didn't prevent the wind rushing through the building. Hill the Cabinet Secretary was struggling to keep his cool and aristocratic veneer. His fists were clenched and frantic, nervous energy radiated from him. His pupils were dilated; despite the cold there was sweat pouring from his brow.

He continued, "Prime Minister, I must protest."

They were surrounded by the portraits of previous occupants of the office; he felt as though they gazed down on them with disapproving eyes.

"There will be severe consequences and not many benefits as far as I can see."

"Hill, I'm not asking you to do this. I'm telling you", he said sternly.

He clenched his fists tighter, attempting to remain calm, but inside he was raging; this action went against everything he believed in.

"But Prime Minister. It's not…."

"This is my decision."

"Have you thought about another option?"

The Prime Minister lifted his head.

"Why not use the knowledge of the Americans' involvement against them?"

"No"

"You could use back channels to show that we know. It could prove useful."

"There must be swift decisive action against this assault on our sovereignty."

"But Prime Minister, the evidence you have is…" he stuttered. "Why would they? It doesn't make sense."

His anger turned to confusion and he simply couldn't understand the Prime Minister's behaviour. Hill was part of the old guard bound by tradition and a sense of duty; this kind of politics broke the unwritten conventions of governing and touched a nerve deep within his psyche.

"I don't know, Hill, but that's not for me to decide. I only have to decide how to respond."

"What if they decide not to leave?"

"We escort them out at gun point."

"But Prime… the pictures, the press. The damage this will do," he said with increasing exasperation.

"What happens if shots are fired?"

"We won't be the first but we'll defend ourselves."

"Prime Minister, this will destroy the *special relationship*."

"That's enough, Hill."

He stopped talking, every fibre of his being wanting to shout, wanted to lash out in some way. But years of maintaining his stiff upper lip prevailed and he didn't give in to his urges. He tightened his fists more tightly until the skin was red and raw but kept his mouth shut.

"Your only job now is to get the civil service on board with this."

He stood rooted to the spot, unsure of what to say next, but didn't comment more. After a few moments he relented, turned on his heel and made his way out of the door, still furious. In the corridor he strode a few paces and ran into Sarah the Prime Minister's PA, who was carrying a stack of briefing documents. Their relationship had always been a little frosty and she tried to get past him as quickly as she could.

"Sarah." She didn't reply, so he tried again. "Sarah."

She stopped, catching the papers as she paused. "Yes."

"You have to go in there and put a stop to this madness."

"It's his decision," she replied.

"I know we haven't always seen eye to eye, Sarah, but please, for the future of our country, just talk to him. He listens to you."

She shook her head and stared at him with fierce eyes. "Hill, he is the Prime Minister. It is his decision."

Hill stamped his foot, suddenly giving in to his anger. "He shouldn't let his personal feelings impact his decision making."

"Careful, Hill."

She immediately knew what he was talking about, the death of Luke, the Prime Minister's son, in Iraq.

"He blames them for it. But he mustn't let that..."

"That's enough, Hill", she said curtly, not angrily just firmly. "He is the Prime Minister; your job is to follow his instructions." She pointed.

"He is making a grave error because he's.."

Sarah felt like she had said enough; she was fuming that Hill would even bring up Luke in their conversation and didn't want to entertain this venting of emotion. She left him in the corridor and made her way into the PM's study.

11:11

Freya

Freya arrived at Sunderland Street, the address provided to her by Simon. She parked her car in the South East corner of the carpark and carefully made her way towards the nearest industrial building. It was in a state of general disrepair and a horrid muddy grey colour; its hollowed frame was dank, dilapidated and dark. In every direction pieces of plaster were falling onto the road and the windows had been smashed. Frozen puddles had formed in the tarmac and she skirted the edge of these, attempting to keep her feet dry. Freya felt reassuringly for her sidearm; her heart beating violently as she peered through a crack in the door. There seemed to be nothing and no one inside.

"Simon, I'm here," she said over the radio.

There was a crackling noise and she repeated, "Simon".

"Yes."

"I'm at the target building."

"OK, let me know how it goes."

"Can you scan the building using the NSA satellite imagery?"

There was a pause and he didn't reply.

'No, Freya, I helped you with the Chinese intercept thing," he said with a sigh. "I can't break chain of command on this."

"Simon, I'm about to enter an unsecured building with no backup."

He didn't say anything and hesitated. "Let me tell H."

"No." She paused. "He'll only get in the way."

"Freya, if they find out about this, there's no way of coming back."

"Look, Simon," she said sharply. "We need to find out if we're being played."

"Freya."

"I'm walking in now. Simon, make your choice."

He hesitated and then breathed out sharply.

"Pulling up thc images now. Standby."

"Thank you."

"You'll have to wait a few minutes - there aren't any satellites."

"Understood."

During the pause Simon said, "Freya, they're going to announce at 12."

"Shit. I thought we would have more time."

Simon continued, "Why are they doing this, Freya? Without the Americans, do they know how many operations will be ru.."

Freya said gently, "I know Simon, I know, and I don't want to think about it."

After a pause she continued, "But we still have time."

He suddenly said, "OK, I got the satellites."

"It's clear."

"Thank you, Simon."

Freya now drew her firearm and proceeded into the building. She was being ultra-cautious and did her normal sectors check and felt for any live traps. The inside of the building was no better than outside. The roof had caved in, big pieces of white plaster had fallen haphazardly to the floor, broken glass littered the outer edges of the room. She ran silently along the east wall being careful to dodge the puddles as she moved.

Then she saw it lit up by the gaping hole in the ceiling, sunlight glinting off its every surface; the evidence she needed to exonerate the Americans. Freya stood there for a full minute and just stared at it. She was terrified; this went a lot deeper than she could have imagined. She thought, 'Fucking shit fuck shit' and for one of the first times in her life she was momentarily unsure what to do.

How could they be so stupid?

After another full minute she made one of the most momentous decisions of her life. It was clear they had discovered one or several top tier traitors and it was crucial that this information didn't fall into the wrong hands. She had to keep this a secret and she couldn't tell MI5. She stood there for another 30 seconds making preparations for what she had to do next. But as she moved forwards, she suddenly heard Simon's frantic voice over the radio. "Freya, get out. Now, get out..." The transmission then became garbled and stopped abruptly.

She hesitated for a moment and then began to sprint, pumping her arms to help her gain momentum, her legs buckling under the exertion. She barged through the door at the far end of the hall, splintering it in many places. She turned the corner and veered right with as much force as she could muster. The explosion sucked all the air out of the room, it started in the centre of the space and then ballooned outward, forcing its way violently towards the street. A shockwave of compressed air and sound blasted forward in every direction and a pillar of fire engulfed the structure. The walls buckled, the windows shattered and the whole building was engulfed in flames.

Freya was blown off her feet.

11:27

Simon

"Who are you speaking to?"

Simon didn't respond - he was shaking violently, terrified for Freya's safety.

"Give me that radio."

Simon was frantically tapping buttons on each panel; he wasn't listening, trying desperately to re-establish contact with Freya.

"You are obligated under Charter paragraph 4 section 2 to hand me that device."

He was sick with worry, holding up the radio now to try to get a signal.

"If you do not comply, I will have to use reasonable force."

Only at this point did he look up and see a burly security official dressed in a finely tailored suit. He had a professional demeanour and didn't look angry, simply moving through the process outlined in his training.

He pleaded, "Please. I need…."

Simon didn't get a chance to finish the sentence as the security officials grabbed his arms and tried to wrest the radio from him.

"Stop…" Simon was wrestling with both of them.

Suddenly H was standing in the doorway just behind Simon's left shoulder. "Who were you speaking to?"

Simon didn't answer, hesitant to get Freya into trouble.

"God damn it. Answer me."

He realised that he had no choice.

"H, you have to send a team to Sunderland Street."

"Why.. what.. Simon…."

"Freya. An explosion."

"What are you talking about?"

Molten anger began to course through him. H's eyes lit up and his nostrils flared. Patches of grey appeared on his forehead but he spoke calmly and deliberately.

"Are you running a live operation without authorisation?"

Simon pleaded again, "H, listen to me. Send a team."

H was breathing forcefully, beating back his temper, trying to slow down a torrent of rage which was now rising in his chest. He looked like he wanted to swear at Simon but he didn't give into temptation and grabbed his phone. Before he dialled it he said threateningly, "I'll deal with you later"

He then turned away and began dialling numbers frantically.

11:32

President Leon

The President sat on the sofa in Claridge's Hotel debating with his National Security Team about the next course of action following their disastrous phone call. His NSA occupied a chair in the middle of the room and had just confirmed that the British were about to announce the expulsion of all American personnel from UK soil. It was a total unmitigated diplomatic disaster, to his left stood Jane Sandai his hard-hitting Secretary of State, ruthlessly intelligent, tough, a competent manager and formidable opponent. She led the dovish part of his cabinet and advocated a wait and see approach. She argued they could respond accordingly to whatever the British eventually decided to do. She said that their intelligence might be off concerning the internal workings of James's government.

To his right sat the American Ambassador to Britain, Ahmad Sod, who was there to give advice about how the UK government worked and what diplomatic levers they might be able to pull. He studied each problem in minute detail and with a finely detailed analytical framework. A career diplomat, he was one of the more measured international appointees and didn't come with any associated political baggage. The President was extremely grateful for this at that moment, he needed clear and rational advice. He smoothed back his brown hair and cleaned his glasses, considering what to advise since unfortunately all the options were bad. Leon was getting angrier and slammed his fist into his hand. They had been going round in circles and the tension was building, none of his advisors could offer a solution to prevent this catastrophe. He stared at them, "Look we have twenty minutes before they announce, we have to do something."

None of them said anything.

"Could we pre-emptively declare our own sanctions? That would at least give us the initiative."

Jane spoke first. "We don't exactly know what they are about to announce so finding the right balance will be difficult."

The President couldn't believe what he was hearing. Finding the right balance, what the hell was she talking about? He was livid. He wanted blood, not to find the right balance. Leon could tell that he was feeling the pressure and tried again to keep calm. But after everything they had done for the British they were about to be kicked in the face, publicly. It made him want to humiliate each and every one of them.

"What about the cabinet?" He enquired.

The Ambassador started, "We've made contact with a few of the most dissident cabinet members. But they are bound by collective responsibility and don't want to resign during a national crisis. James's government looks stable for the moment."

"Surely the House of Commons thinks this is a terrible idea?"

He continued, "They haven't been informed yet."

He began to pace frustratedly, his team was failing him and with each option closed down it made him even more furious.

"I'm going to go to Downing Street."

His Secret Service chief spoke now. "Sir, we're in lockdown. For your safety we can't leave this building."

He suddenly lost his cool. "Arrrg," he exclaimed and began angrily pacing the room again. He then stood for thirty seconds before saying, "Helen, get Hill back on the line."

11:39

Isaiah

The sun had now risen sufficiently that they could see without artificial light. Isaiah and Daniel were busy preparing for the next stage in the operation. In the middle of the room they sat haphazardly, each struggling to find a space for them to work without interfering with the others. The cushions and pillows were pushed to one side to give them more space. Isaiah hated this chaos but it wasn't a priority to organise it at the moment. They began a well-planned process, carefully sealing the boxes, burying any electronic trails they had left, destroying hard drives. To his left and right, a number of men were building an assortment of devices, bits of wire and tools spread around them. As Daniel was struggling with one of the final screws in his device Isaiah lent towards him.

"She triggered the explosion." He pulled out a tablet and showed Daniel the video.

They both watched as Freya entered the warehouse, skirted the outer walls, waited for two minutes, answered her radio and then ran as fast as she could for the exit. A few seconds later the entire building collapsed into a fireball, dust, plaster and debris littering the car park.

They both looked at each other deeply confused; it didn't make any sense.

"Why?"

Isaiah shrugged his shoulders.

"What game is she playing?" Again Isaiah didn't know.

"I always told you she was a liability." Daniel said, shaking his head.

Isaiah now spoke for the first time, "Is she injured?"

"I can't tell - we don't have a camera on the outside."

"What are you going to do?"

11:41

Freya

Bits of twisted metal fell to the ground in all directions, the vibration of dropping objects echoed throughout the car park, clouds of dust were billowing outwards from the bomb crater into the sky. Freya lay in the middle of this surrounded by debris, her head buzzing, her ears ringing violently, disorientated by the wall of sound following the explosion.

She struggled to regain consciousness, retching, grasping around for something stationery to pull her upright. She ingested a breath of air filled with ash and dirt and started coughing violently. Reality was fluid and unstable; she passed out again.

Sometime later, she was awoken by a clattering sound. Her vision was blurry but she could see a mechanical device to her left that beeped with increasing shrillness. She realised slowly that she was in the back of an ambulance; she felt a sharp scratch as she was hooked up to a drip and only then did she regain most of her faculties.

"What are you doing?"

"I'm putting some IV fluid in and taking you to hospital."

"No"

"What?"

"Take this stuff off me."

She began attempting to take the needle out of her arm and began wrestling with the medic.

"Miss, you've been badly….," said the medic, attempting to restrain her. "We need to take you to hospital."

She stopped struggling and held up her finger, "Firstly, never ever call me miss and secondly, I'm refusing treatment." She started forward and winched in pain. Shooting pains coursed through her left side and her muscles spasmed.

She gasped but tried desperately not to show any pain. The medic let go and said "You need to…" Freya took out the IV and wrenched open the door.

She hobbled out of the ambulance, her legs buckling as she stepped out. The medic called after her, "Stop…. What are you doing?"

She began searching her pockets for her phone. She finally located it inside her left jacket pocket. It had a huge crack in the screen and the buttons were badly damaged. She tried to activate the screen, which flickered for a few moments but then died.

Freya shouted, "Fuck" and threw it to the ground.

She walked over to a group of MET police officers. "You." She pointed to the older looking gentlemen. "Are you in charge?"

"Yes."

"Give me your phone."

"What?"

"Give me your phone right now, unless you want to explain to the

Prime Minister directly that he is committing the biggest foreign policy disaster of the 21st century."

The officer looked to his comrades. When they didn't say anything, he handed her the phone and she dialled memorised numbers, calling H directly.

"Yes."

"H, this is Freya."

"You!!" he exclaimed, "If you try and pull another stunt like that, I'll have you arrested."

"Yes," she said ignoring his comment. He continued, "Is that understood?"

"Yes," she continued before he could interrupt her again. "H, the Prime Minister is making a terrible mistake."

"What are you talking about?"

"The press conference, the expulsion."

He paused and said, "Do you have any proof?"

"No. But you need to call him right now. The press conference is in 10 minutes."

"So you want me to dial the Prime Minister, risk my entire career with no hard evidence, with just your word as an assurance?" he scoffed.

"H, stop arse covering and do the right thing."

His voice filled with menace, "You know what, Freya, I am about this close to dragging you in here myself."

"Fine", she shouted and hung up the phone.

She took some deep breaths; the cool air was working, gradually bringing down her heart rate with each gulp and making her feel more relaxed. She desperately needed a clear head but it took her a full two minutes to calm down. She typed a new number, one that she was never supposed to have.

It rang three times and was answered by Sarah, who sounded very stressed and answered hurriedly, "Hello".

"Hi, this is Doctor Thornberry from Westminster hospital, is it possible to speak to the Prime Minister?"

"What's it about?"

"His daughter."

"I'm sorry but he's about to go into a press conference, is it possible for you to call back later?"

"No, I'm afraid it's urgent."

She sounded reluctant but then walked a few paces towards the Prime Minister. She whispered, "Hospital, your daughter."

"Is everything OK?" He answered the phone and sounded very worried.

"Richard, this is Freya."

She used his first name to remind him of their personal relationship, she hoped this might allow him to listen to her.

"Freya, how did you get this number?" He sounded very upset. "You can't call me like this."

"I know, Prime Minister and I'm sorry, but I had no choice."

She now used his official title as a sign of respect, hoping that it would make him listen to her next few words.

"What?"

"I think that the evidence you have concerning American involvement in the attacks today has been fabricated."

"Do you have any proof of this?"

"Yes, but nothing concrete. But I can get some, just delay the press conference."

"Look, Freya, I will always appreciate everything you have done for my daughter over the years and you've always been a great friend to her."

He paused. "But I can't delay unless you give me some hard evidence."

She continued more desperately now, "What we dreamed of and spoke about before, it can't happen now."

She knew the significance of what she had said but he didn't reply. It was hugely risky on a phone that could be monitored.

He simply said, "Freya. I have to go."

"Richard, I covered..."

She was interrupted by an aide who entered the Prime Minister's room and said, "We're ready for you now."

He nodded vigorously, held up his hand and began to end the call. "Goodbye Freya."

"Prime Minister, Richard, think … "

He hung up the phone.

The Prime Minister stood there furrowing his brow, as the world's media waited outside, all straining to get the best position for their pictures. Camera flashes lit up the back wall as he waited to go inside. He rocked forwards and backwards on the spot struggling under the weight of this choice.

PART 2

Walking a tightrope

12:00 to 13:00 PM

Prime Minister James

James stood in front of the rows of photographers, shuffling his papers and readying himself to begin his speech. Flashes of strobe illuminated the scene; he tried not to blink as he looked out towards the cameras.

"It is with a heavy heart that I am making this speech today."

He paused, he looked visibly upset and stopped for a moment looking down. He only just managed to keep his composure as he turned back towards the camera.

"Our good friend and colleague Faisal Jarvis was shot and killed today in a cowardly and disgusting attack. Those who committed this act of savagery will be met with the full force of the law and we will not rest until we find those responsible. I want to pay tribute to Faisal, a dedicated family man, public servant and personal friend. We will never forget his dedication to public service and unflinching duty to this nation. We must also thank the police, first responders and armed forces who take enormous risks to keep us safe every day. Your professionalism and self-sacrifice are examples to us all."

He paused now, stared directly into the camera and emphasised the next few words, abandoning his notes.

"We will NEVER give in to this terrorism."

He continued reading the teleprompter, "An investigation has already started." He paused, "and after consulting with the National Security Council and the Independent Unit for Intelligence Analysis, it has been concluded that elements of the United States intelligence services gave direct material support to this attack."

There were gasps in the audience and the journalists began scribbling notes frantically.

"This represents an unlawful use of force on British territory and will be met with a swift and robust response. We will share this evidence with our counterparts in the United States and if we do not receive a satisfactory answer within 12 hours, I am ordering that all American diplomats and military personnel must leave British soil immediately."

Freya was watching the press conference on the borrowed phone and she dropped her head in her hands. "Fuck", she said under her breath, "aaaaaw." The disappointment and anger poured out of her as she held her head: she had failed.

12:14

Isaiah

Isaiah and Daniel sat with their backs against the wall drinking tea, summoning the courage for the next stage in the operation. After some time Daniel asked,

"How long are we waiting here?"

"Until we are ready."

It was a typically cryptic response from Isaiah, who never revealed many details of a plan until the last moment.

"Are you ready for this?"

Daniel thought for a moment and then nodded his head. "Yes."

He stood back, glad to see Isaiah's confidence return; it put him at ease. The whole team sat in a circle in the centre of the room. They linked hands and began to pray, asking for the strength to do what they had to. They entreated God that, should they be killed, he would send their soul straight to heaven. They sat like this for some time, it was hard to be sure how long, swaying in rhythmic cycles, strengthening the resolve of all the men who gathered. They stopped, stood praying, then prostrated before the almighty one final time, before picking up their weapons and gathering by the door.

It was their moment.

12:27

Freya

Back at Thames House H and Freya were arguing in his office.

"Freya, we need to talk about your conduct. If we were not in a national crisis I would relieve you immediately."

Freya was musing, deep in thought, and barely heard the words.

"Something doesn't make sense here," she muttered.

"Did you hear what I said?"

He stared at her, wanting her to capitulate to his will, but she wouldn't give him the satisfaction.

"That bomb was remote detonated," she began.

"Why does that matter?"

She gave him a withering look. "Because that means they knew I was coming."

"It could have been a pressure switch."

"I don't think so. There were too many entrances and it didn't explode when I stepped on something; the explosion was remotely detonated…."

"What about surveillance?"

"I did a sectors check and I had a signal jammer operational at the time."

He raised his eyebrows and said nothing.

"Probably it was an undetectable device," he said, ignoring her previous comment.

She didn't respond, just folded her arms and felt upset again that he wasn't listening to her.

"Freya, I'm demoting you."

"What? Why?" Suddenly Freya was alert to his words.

"You have shown an inability to follow instructions and you led a dangerous mission by yourself, with no oversight and no backup."

"From now on you must respect the chain of command."

Freya wasn't really listening and didn't care about the demotion; she was working the problem in her head.

"Listen, H. We need to do an immediate Agent Screening Exam and we need to pick up James Reynolds."

H's eyebrows rose to the top of his head; it was clear he had no interest in performing an agent screening exam. "Freya, what are you talking about?" he said, startled. "We can't just start randomly harassing diplomats."

"Look, we can't do much more diplomatic damage. We just announced that we are expelling their diplomatic mission."

"I won't even consider it." He shook his head.

Freya stamped her foot in frustration, boiling anger was filling her brain with disgust at what she thought was his intransigence and stupidity.

"H, do you want to be remembered as the director general who took action when his country was attacked or do you want to be remembered as the leader who capitulated as wave after wave of devastation brought us to our knees?"

He ignored the last sentences and said these words very slowly:

"Freya if you ever… EVER…. speak to me that way again. I will have you immediately escorted out of the building in handcuffs." He paused and tapped the desk with his finger. "You will work with the analytics team to search the CCTV for any clues pending an inquiry."

"But H…"

He interrupted, "Now get out of my office, Freya. You're dismissed." A guard appeared at Freya's shoulder and put a hand on her shoulder.

"Get your hands off me," she retorted, sharply brushing his hand away.

He released the hand and like an irate child she slammed the door as hard as she could as she exited. She walked out into the corridor and into the bathroom, slamming her fist into the other hand - a habit that she had when she was livid with anger. She focused on a number of breathing exercises the therapist had taught her to use when she was furious. She screamed as loudly as she could, slamming the door shut, letting the emotion rush out of her. Gradually she felt better and thought darkly, they'll see what I'm capable of.

More composed now she walked back into the corridor. As she was re-entering the Terminal, Fatima was striding towards her with a broad grin, inviting Freya to walk towards her. Freya's mood shifted abruptly as Fatima came closer.

"We found them."

12:40

President Leon

"We need a response."

The President was surrounded by his core team, everyone superfluous had been barred from entering, they needed focused attention and smooth decision making. Only Jane Sandai, Ahmad Sod and Shane Dilalio remained seated in a semi-circle with a few assorted staffers taking notes. They represented the branches of government that were crucial to any response to this crisis. Shane had operational authority over the intelligence branches, Jane would head up the State department and Ahmad would handle the domestic implications in the UK.

Ahmad and Shane sat in several chairs opposite the sofa. Jane was the first to speak, perched on the edge of the main cushion, "We can begin evacuations but it will take us much more than 24 hours, Sir. There are a number of pieces of heavy equipment to…"

Leon interrupted her. "We're not leaving."

Shane spoke now, "Sir, their military is being mobilised and they've almost got the House of Commons…"

Again the President interrupted him. "We're not leaving; we've done nothing wrong."

His advisors looked at each other, not sure what to make of this. There was awkward silence for thirty seconds and Ahmad was the first to break it.

"Do you have a plan?" They all looked at him.

He said again very slowly, "We are NOT leaving."

Jane spoke now, "This could lead to a stand-off, this could get very messy very quickly. It could look like we are bullying a smaller country, one of our closest, most loyal allies."

"I don't give a shit about the political implications. This is not right. We've guaranteed their security for years, we've saved their asses multiple times and this is the thanks we get. Screw that."

The advisors looked at each other and no one said anything. The decision was his and they had tried to talk sense into him. The President changed tack, calming down slightly.

"But we need a response."

He turned to Jane and Ahmad. "As a first step I want you to cancel all bilateral scientific work, intelligence cooperation, suspend the five eyes arrangement and sanction key ministers."

There were shocked looks from his staff.

Shane spoke with exasperation, "Sir, we have almost a dozen ongoing intelligence operations with British involvement. This would mean obliterating months of work and would severely damage our national security."

The President nodded, finally listening again and less emotional. "OK, I want you to suspend cooperation on any future security partnerships."

He then continued, "Jane, can you draft the order for me to check? We have to get this out there as quickly as possible; the American people will expect a swift response."

Jane nodded and asked only one question, "Do you want to extend the order to any American company with a large British shareholding? Or simply government funded research?"

He answered quickly, "government funded research."

The advisors began writing notes. "Ahmad get your team to draft a press release for the media agencies in the UK. Tell them that unless the British government rescinds this order there will be further consequences and this is only the first stage."

Ahmad replied, "That might sound quite threatening, Sir. You may want to…"

Leon pointed to the group and suddenly lost his temper. "WE are not the problem here; those arseholes ARE HUMILATING US in front of the whole world. We CANNOT let them do this to us."

12:50

Freya

Freya's team sat in the conference room waiting for their briefing. She was getting fidgety with every passing minute, but this meeting was critical, it would tell her who the enemy was and more crucially what their weaknesses were. By now they had identified Daniel Massoud, a well-known member of the Knights of Christ, an extremist Christian organisation in Egypt. He was a close associate to Isaiah Beshara (The Scorpion) a famous terrorist who the Egyptian government had been trying to track down for years.

As soon as the first attacker had been confirmed, the duty officer had called everyone in the NSC to find out if we had any subject matter experts on the pre-approved list. They were quickly found and requisitioned from MI6 across the river. The members of the new task force strode into the room and Freya was relieved that her wait was finally over. She desperately wanted to get out the office and begin tracking their cell down.

Richard Armitage their frontman was the head of MI6's Egypt desk and also deputy policy director for the Middle East. He had the air of someone who was well trained in the art of diplomacy, taking his time to shake everyone's hands when he entered the room. But Freya also understood that he was someone who had clearly seen the uglier side of life. There was a certain sharpness to his eyes and mannerisms that betrayed this fact. She didn't know much about him but guessed from his posture and demeanour that he had a military background, the same as most senior members of 6. He handed out a report and several other prominent members of MI5 entered the room including Sir Malcolm Harris the GCHQ liaison and Tariq Makar of Special Forces Joint Intelligence.

When everyone was settled down, he stood up and switched on the projector. He started with a picture of the Coptic Cross; it was a mix of the pharaonic symbol of life and an orthodox Christian cross curved at the top. "By now you all know that we've identified Daniel and Isaiah as the culprits for today's attack. Our role here today is to give you more of an insight into how they think, what their background is and how they operate. This should help us make better predictions about their next moves and also gauge the extent of their operation here in London."

He paused, showing a picture of a church in Cairo. "Just to give some background on the Coptics in Egypt. They are the oldest church in the world and have been practising Christianity for around 1800 years."

He turned to the next slide. "They were introduced to the new faith by Saint Mark in the first century and the church was probably expanded by another missionary named Apollos, although the evidence for this is patchy. Up until about 1000 years ago Egypt was a predominantly Christian country after which for political and demographic reasons Islam became the dominant religion."

The next picture showed a population chart, "Today Coptics make up 8% of the population." He paused. "Historically, relations between the two religions have been peaceful with occasional clashes. But things have deteriorated in the last few decades as a response to a number of

Islamist bombing campaigns against churches. In retaliation, there have been attacks against Egyptian security forces and Islamic targets."

He turned to the next slide. "The Knights of Christ first came to our attention back in 1997 during the massacre in Luxor. 62 tourists were killed and it was one of the deadliest attacks on foreigners in Egyptian history."

He briefly showed photos of mutilated bodies and blood spread around the ancient tombs of Luxor.

"After this atrocity, there was a huge outpouring of grief for the victims. Although protesting is banned in Egypt there were a few ways in which ordinary Egyptians could show their anger. There was a revolutionary song written by a popular band in Cairo and many held up photos to remember the dead. However, amongst the Christian population we saw a different reaction."

He turned to the next slide - it was of graffiti, a blood red cross.

"We started to see this sign repeated in the streets of Alexandria. This is one of the more liberal parts of Egypt and it has a larger Coptic Christian population. Authorities quickly removed the sign but then it started springing up everywhere - in leaflets at churches, on walls, on the internet."

The presentation continued with a photo showing priests being taken away in handcuffs. "For some time things were quiet, but then in 2003 several prominent church leaders were imprisoned for allowing the sign in their churches and meetings of a banned political organisation called the Coptic Circle. It was demanding that Christians be allowed to govern their own affairs and be free of police brutality."

The next image showed a group of men blocking an entrance to a church. "These arrests didn't have the effect the authorities hoped. Sit-ins occurred in churches, blocking security forces from removing the sign of the Coptic Circle. There were beatings and arrests; several protesters were killed."

He turned to the next slide; angry protesters could be seen in all directions - including many women in headscarves from the Islamic community. "The protests grew and the Egyptian government backed down. They prevented security forces from entering churches and they allowed the sign of the Coptic Circle to remain. After this, things were again quiet for some time."

He gestured towards another man who Freya hadn't noticed earlier. "At this point, I'm going to hand over to Adrian."

Adrian stood up and took the position vacated by Richard. He seemed very nervous, his hands were shaking and he was very careful with where he placed his feet. Clearly he wasn't a fan of public speaking.

"Thank you," he said, his voice shaking.

He began stumbling with the words and breathed to steady himself. "A few years later we began to see this man appear in the promotional material for the Coptic Circle."

He showed a picture of a young man with sharp eyebrows. "It was only when he changed the name of the Coptic Circle to the Knights of Christ that we really realised his importance." As he continued he seemed to gain more confidence. Freya really empathised with how he was feeling; she sat up straighter and looked more attentive, trying to encourage him.

He turned to another slide, showing a number of men and women sitting in a circle. "He began holding meetings - arguing that it wasn't possible for Muslims and Christians to live together. At first there was little support for his aims and his group was small."

The next slide showed a line of people waiting to be fed. "He started feeding the very poorest Christians and petitioning the government to help with economic development in Christian areas; he was ignored by the military."

He continued to a picture of Isaiah preaching from the pulpit. "His groups started to grow. He argued that it wasn't possible for Coptics to live in an Islamic state as a minority and that they must build a new country called Christendom - a place free of Islamic oppression."

He paused and added, "Most well-educated Christians scorned him for causing trouble but he retained significant support among poorer Coptics."

He continued, "After much debate the Egyptian government decided to put increasing amounts of pressure on the organisation. They made being part of the Knights of Christ a criminal offence and arrested many of its supporters. Security forces went into churches and forcefully removed many priests and worshippers."

After a temporary spike in confidence Adrian started to lose his flow. "There were beatings and photos were beamed around the country of screaming teenagers being dragged from churches. They narrowly missed capturing Isaiah."

His voice became even more jarring. "These photos prompted widespread protests and this time the government was not so lenient."

He stopped and Richard asked, "Adrian, are you OK? He breathed deeply to compose himself, which seemed to work, his voice becoming more settled. Freya really felt for him and was glad to see him continue.

"Yes, I'm fine." He paused. "I'll continue."

The moment had passed and he turned to the next slide. "The army opened fire on a group of teenage protesters, killing all of them. At the same time there were attacks by Islamic extremists on churches, which further angered the Coptic community."

He didn't change slides but spoke to the audience. "They felt that the mostly Muslim security forces didn't protect them but protected the extremists and at this point the Knights of Christ turned in a more radical direction. Isaiah advocated the overthrow of the Egyptian government - only then could he found his new state. Violence was now part of the group's constitution, but his supporters were few."

He showed a police picture of the aftermath of a car bomb. "The first attack carried out by the Knights of Christ was on a police check point in 2008. No one was killed but two police officers were injured. In response, the government redoubled its efforts; they managed to arrest Isaiah and crush the young organisation. All major supporters were arrested; churches known to be sympathetic to the cause were taken over by security forces and the meetings stopped. At this point the government thought it had succeeded and for three years things died down."

He turned to the next slide which showed a map of the Middle East. "In 2010 the Arab spring which started in Tunisia spread to Egypt; thousands lined the streets campaigning for social justice. This all resulted in the 2011 revolution, which was a major turning point for the Knights of Christ. As the chaos spread Isaiah escaped from jail and came back as a hero ready to lead the cause. His status was further elevated by several church leaflets and radio broadcasts which exalted his character. Bomb attacks on churches by Islamic radicals rallied many to his cause."

He turned to the next slide showing pictures of the aftermath of several attacks. "The Knights of Christ carried out several more attacks, each of them successful, and there was a greater sense of urgency as Mohammed Mosi, the Egyptian President, tried to pass what many saw as an Islamist constitution. The chaos allowed more attacks against Coptics which included an assassination campaign targeting priests. More and more were buying into Isaiah's vision of Christendom. Previously sceptical Coptics were inspired by the idea of running their own affairs."

He clicked the remote again and showed a graphic of the timeline of their attacks. "Since 2013 there have been many attacks against military and Islamic targets, all of them successful. In the last five years the Knights have widened the scope of their bombing campaign to include targets that might disrupt American and British military aid to the government. A good example of this is the 2014 bombing of the port in Alexandria through which supplies of weapons were transferred to the Egyptian Armed Forces."

He paused and pointed towards the pages in their hands.

"A full breakdown is available in the report. They must have a significant network of support in London, but we lack any significant intelligence on their cell."

He paused and nodded to them, happy to have regained control of the situation. "Any questions?"

Sir Malcolm Harris (Operations chief) started, "How are they funded?"

"Our intelligence is patchy although there are some general indications."

Everyone in the room had been given a copy of the report and he asked them to look at it. "If you turn to page 39 of the report, it contains a breakdown of who we believe to be their major financiers."

There was a shuffling of pages as everyone turned to the required page and he enlarged a photo on the screen. "This man, Nathan Ambrosia, is a major supporter in terms of tactical support and finance. Former Lord's Resistance Army, he was a major player in Joseph Kony's shadow government."

"How do they get money into the country?"

"We're not sure, possibly using diamonds, jewellery or packets of cash. International wire transfers are too risky and the mail is too unreliable. He must have a courier but we haven't identified them yet."

"How do you know he's directly funding them?"

"If you turn to page 41." Again you could hear the shuffling of paper. "The CIA intercepted a large number of phone calls between Nathan and Isaiah; in each they discussed money and logistics."

"That seems like a careless mistake to make."

"Not necessarily; each call was made between a payphone and a different sim card: very difficult to track. The CIA had to use IMSTA with voice recognition to find the communication between them."

He nodded, satisfied with this answer. IMSTA was a top-secret data collection programme that tapped into the mobile phone network and hoovered up massive amounts of data. It then used machine learning, pattern recognition and artificial intelligence to flag anything suspicious, which was then scrutinised by an Intelligence analyst.

He continued and enlarged another photo on the screen of an internet profile with the name superchristian156. "If you would like to turn to page 42, you can see that they have financial backers in other parts of the world. We intercepted several large payments made to an account in Cairo controlled by the Knights of Christ. The money was rerouted through a series of shell companies via Bermuda but we believe the origin to be the United States. If I were to make an educated guess, I would say that the most likely suspects are some of the more radical evangelical churches in the southern United States. They also seem to have backers in the UK, the..."

At that moment he stopped talking as the door swung open and Simon raced into the room. He came in and blurted out, "We've pinged their phones."

Immediate excitement gripped the attendees and the briefing came to an unceremonious end, as they dodged coffee cups, chairs and other bodies in their hurry to escape the room. They piled back into the corridor and into the Terminal, desperate to track Isaiah's location.

13:00 to 14:00 PM

Freya

Freya was angry. After the initial excitement of pinging the suspect's phone they had rushed back into the terminal but quickly realised that it was a false alarm. Now everyone had returned to their desks ashen faced and Simon was sitting in embarrassed silence.

Martin walked along the corridor briskly with a man Freya didn't recognise. "Freya, this is Alexander Hammer."

Alexander stretched out his hand but Freya turned back to her computer.

"I'm busy."

"He's your new five eyes liaison."

"I didn't ask for one."

"He's been assigned to you."

Freya was immediately angry and looked towards her new charge ashen-faced. This action mixed two of the things she hated most, bureaucracy and management. At that moment H entered the Terminal and was heading towards his office. She marched up towards him.

"Did you authorise this?" she said accusingly before he had time to speak.

He replied and held up a hand. "I don't want to hear it, Freya." He paused, "You are to keep the Americans fully updated on your progress."

He emphasised the word fully to give it special significance. She hated how she was being patronised.

"H, I don't need a babysitter."

"You have no choice in the matter, keep Alexander in the loop," he said and continued towards the door.

Freya thought, the Americans must be leaning on the British government very hard if they asked for a man on the grid. In fact, she was shocked that they were still cooperating in national security policy areas.

She hated this, really hated it. The last thing she needed was someone getting in her way.

As she came back to her workstation, she commanded him, "OK, you sit there and don't touch anything."

He nodded and placed his briefcase on the desk.

"Are you going to ask me to do anything?"

"No."

He looked at her sternly. "I am here on orders of the President to make sure that the investigation is carried out promptly and professionally."

Freya wasn't listening and replied, "OK".

"I can be of use."

Freya thought, I need to distract this guy with something - he was clearly someone who needed to be doing something in order to feel comfortable.

"OK, if you want to be useful, take a look at these interview transcripts and tell me what you see."

Across government departments the same ebb and flow of bilateral relationships continued despite the intentions of their political masters.

It was one of the great contradictions of international relations. With her liaison distracted, Freya turned her attention to escaping. She couldn't be trapped in here; she knew what she needed to do to get the job done. She decided that she couldn't keep playing by the rules, it was getting them nowhere. She strode towards the back of the building determined to escape as quickly as she could. She started looking cautiously from left to right, wanting as few as possible to observe her and hoping her absence would go unnoticed for some time. She walked briskly to the back of the building where it was quieter, glancing behind her. At the back door, she tried her key card, but it flashed red and wouldn't work.

She was confused.

The security official asked her, "Would you like me to try?"

Freya nodded, indicating to him to proceed. He took the card and tried the door again; it still wouldn't move and he said, "Let me check."

He put the card against a tablet computer and said, "It seems that your permissions have changed; you can access most of the internal rooms but can't leave the building without permission."

She smiled and thought, well played H. She nodded and indicated that she needed her card back. Developing a new plan, she made her way along the left side of the main conference room, dodging most of the computers. No one noticed her, engrossed in their work. She pivoted on her axis, turned a corner and quickly traversed the main corridor. She walked past the main complex of the Terminal and knocked on the door of Simon's office. He was now upstairs away from the mainframe, but he saw her through the window and waved at her to enter.

"Are you OK?"

He lifted his head, "I'm fine. Are you?"

She nodded, "I didn't properly thank you for saving me back there. I really appreciate it."

He waved away the comment. "You would have done the same for me."

They looked at each other for a moment, some tension hanging between them.

He continued, "But we need to speak. You can't pressurise me like that."

"I know. I'm sorry I… just really want to know the truth."

"I understand. But H has given me an official warning and confined me here."

"I'm sorry, Simon."

He joked, "And I was hoping to have a career here."

They both smiled and looked at each other. "You and me both." She paused and added, "I'm not sure we're cut out for that."

"Speak for yourself."

They laughed and their eyes locked. But their chat, the airing of issues and their joke seemed to have strengthened and reset their friendship. Freya pushed the conversation in a different direction, "Simon, we can't find out anything here, we have to get out."

He looked nervously left and right as though checking no one was listening. "I agree. But they've suspended our passes."

She smiled, "I have a plan."

13:15

Isaiah

The small convoy traversed the narrow streets of Croydon, disguising themselves in regular vehicles which travelled slowly. They passed crowds of tourists, all busying themselves with visits to the great gleaming archways of Britain's colonial past. Despite the recent attack, these travellers seemed completely unaware of the chaos ensuing on London Bridge just a few miles away. They were here on holiday and clearly wanted to enjoy their getaway. Isaiah and Daniel were in the lead car driven by one of their fighters. Daniel was upset with what he thought was Isaiah's refusal to see who the real enemy was.

"Our priority should be *il kafir"* (the unholy one)

"No, we have a plan."

"The Egyptian government they …," he struggled to say it, "we should …,"

"Daniel," Isaiah's voice filled with malice. "We will not speak of this again."

"This is a waste of time."

Isaiah interrupted and said, not angrily but very firmly, "We cannot have Christendom while NATO give billions in military aid to prop up the Islamic government - they will always overpower us."

Daniel fell silent.

"Daniel, we have no choice."

The car was silent. He wanted to object but he didn't; he would follow Isaiah anywhere and trusted his command. But he felt differently, deep down he viscerally hated *il kafir.* He still had nightmares of the revolution, the mutilated bodies ripped apart by automatic rounds, the pools of blood collecting on the pavement, the terrified screams of mothers cradling their children. He hated the Muslims for what they had done.

Checking the mirror nervously, he continued watching out for any tails. They parked in an adjacent road for some time making sure they weren't being followed. After knowing it was safe to proceed, they drove another kilometre and pulled up outside a non-descript fish and chips shop. To its left was a dilapidated SPAR shop where a few jostling kids were buying sweets; apart from that the street was completely deserted. Isaiah turned to the men in the back of the car.

"We're here."

13:33

Prime Minister James

The Prime Minister was preparing his speech when there was a knock on the door. Sarah said, "Prime Minister, you have Harry from the Whips office waiting for you."

"Can you ask him to come back later?"

"He says it is urgent."

The Prime Minister hesitated for a moment and then nodded.

He stood up from behind his desk and walked to the door to shake Harry's hand.

"Harry, what can I do for you?" He tried to be cordial even though he resented the interruption.

"Prime Minister, I'm afraid that I have some very grave news."

He didn't interrupt. "There is a lot of disquiet within the party. There is a formal no confidence motion being submitted to Sir Bradley as we speak."

James nodded, not surprised, but annoyed. He asked simply, "Do they have the votes?"

"It will be close."

His temper getting the better of him, he said sharply, "Well you'd better find out then."

Harry looked taken aback by this and said nothing. The Prime

Minister returned to his speech and looked up, saying, "Come back here when you know."

Harry said nothing but nodded, turned on his heel and left. James ruffled his brow again; he tried to concentrate on his speech but found it difficult. The party was already covering their backsides, disassociating themselves from his tainted brand. It was to be expected, but it still annoyed him how fickle they all were. During one of the greatest crises this country had ever faced, instead of confronting the situation head-on they were already playing the blame game. He thought darkly, if this is to be the end of me, I'm not going down quietly.

13:44

Freya

Freya grabbed her key card from her pocket and squatted down next to Simon's computer.

"What are you doing?" Simon asked.

"I'm looking for your hard drive."

"Why?"

She began rubbing her key card with the back of the computer, it pained him to see his precious computer used this way but he resisted the urge to say anything.

"Do you think that will work?"

"Should do."

They carefully peered through the window to check that the corridor was clear. Leaving Simon's office, they made their way out onto the walkway to a separate part of the building. Freya strode up to the security office at the end of the corridor.

Freya walked in and said politely, with a smile, "Hi, my key card isn't working. Can you check it for me?"

She passed the security official the card and she ran it over a terminal.

She said, "It's been corrupted."

"Aww no." She pretended to look annoyed.

Before being prompted the security woman said, "Don't worry, I can give you this temporary pass for the moment, but you'll have to order a new one."

Freya nodded, "OK, understood."

The security official handed her a form, Freya signed the form and handed it back. The official then passed her a new card with the string attached. Surprised that it had been that easy, Freya indicated to Simon to follow her.

They both made their way into the corridor. Freya said to Simon quietly, "We can't go out the front entrance." She paused, "Where's your car?"

"Basement level 2."

They looked left and right, then traversed the central atrium, seeing no one of consequence, and raced down several flights of stairs. They walked slowly in places where they might be observed, speeding up in the quieter sections. Reaching the door that led to the underground car park they were abruptly stopped in their tracks. Fatima stood in front of them, her arms folded.

"Where are you going?"

"We're following up a lead." Freya tried to speak as unsuspiciously as she could.

"I want to come."

"Thank you, Fatima, but we're OK."

"Freya, we're a team. We work together, we always have each other's backs. I want to help."

Freya's heart swelled with pride.

"It could be dangerous."

She nodded resolutely. "I know the risks."

As they stood in the corridor in a lopsided triangle, Freya could hear voices behind them and made her decision quickly.

She nodded. "OK. Let's go."

Being careful to move as quietly as they could, the unlikely trio continued down to the car park door. Freya grabbed her key card and tried to use it to open the door, but the terminal continued to flash red.

"Shit." She tried it again but it wouldn't budge. She still didn't have access to the external doors; they must have given her the same permissions on the new card as the old one.

Fatima intervened now. "Let me try."

Freya moved to the left and Fatima darted forward, presented her card to the control panel and the door flashed green. Relieved, they looked over their shoulders and quickly hurried into the car park. It was a dismal place, full of 60s concrete that had seen much better days. Several broken lights flickered and it was in a general state of disrepair. Parts of the ceiling insulation were visible to the left and there was damp seeping through the walls. They turned a corner and entered Simon's battered silver Toyota Corolla. Simon started the engine and they sped past the car park's first pillar. There was a loud bang as an entry door to the car park was violently closed; someone was running and shouting. Freya thought, "Shit, they must have seen us on camera."

The figure was several paces behind them, running full tilt.

"Maybe we should stop?" Simon asked tentatively.

Freya shook her head vigorously, "Go, go."

The man continued to chase them, but they were moving too fast; he was red faced and screaming, "Stop, you must stop."

Freya and Simon exchanged looks of fear as the barrier to the carpark began to close.

Fatima yelled, "We won't fit."

Freya said, "Don't stop, Simon."

Simon pressed his foot down more sharply on the accelerator as the barrier came down.

It was only metres away.

14:00 to 15:00 PM

Trident41

Trident sat alone back in his apartment, feeling awful.

"What have I done?"

He thought that he could help SUEZ, do what needed to be done and then disappear into retirement. But now it was clear they had lost control, and those Christian maniacs were in charge. He hadn't wanted any of this and now Isaiah was running around causing mayhem in London. He had long ago forgotten about ethics, he was now willing to do whatever it took to build Christendom. In his mind any means justified the ends.

He let his face be swallowed by his hands. He thought, 'I must do something.'

He couldn't let his coding be used for something so barbaric again. Brick Fish must be rendered unusable. Trident loved this country and he didn't want to see British citizens killed. He was doing this for the love of a place that he didn't want to see led astray by those awful Neocons in the American government.

Yes, he thought again, we need to get the Americans out of this country. But we don't need to completely reorder the balance of global power and we don't need to kill thousands of my fellow countrymen. The Foreign Secretary might have been a necessary evil, but any more was unnecessary. It couldn't and shouldn't be allowed.

He was sweating and struggling with the idea, what should I do?

He fired up his computer and began logging in. The first stage, Trident felt, was to find out what they had done to his coding and if they planned to use Brick Fish again. He sat back in his chair and became totally absorbed by his computer.

14:18

Freya

Freya, Simon and Fatima had made it out largely unscathed, their car now bearing a few large scratches to the roof. They waited outside the embassy near Vauxhall bridge, where there was light afternoon traffic: a few motorists were using this break between rush hour to journey home. The sun was starting to dip now, its pale rays filtering over the wall in front of them. Fatima had chosen to stay in Simon's car monitoring the communication data; Simon and Freya waited behind a wall.

Simon looked nervous, "Are you sure about this, Freya?"

"No." She smiled.

He shook his head, wondering about how he found himself in these situations. There was something about Freya, a magnetic pull that he found difficult to resist. Maybe it was love, maybe it was respect. Simon had never been in love and wasn't exactly sure what it was or felt like. He wondered if this was it? He would do almost anything for her without any regard for himself. His caution, selfishness and rationality were going straight out of the window.

They waited, their bodies taut. Simon looked at his phone again and watched the CCTV from outside the embassy. It should capture the moment that the car left the car park.

This would give them about 45 seconds warning.

They were breaking so many laws Simon had lost count, and he became more and more anxious as time passed. He attempted to console himself with the thought that they could attempt to stop the car using the police powers act, which technically gave them permission to do this on an officially sanctioned operation. But this was unsanctioned. He shook his head, H would probably claim responsibility for this. But maybe he wouldn't, would he? I don't know. The stream of negative thoughts continued unabated.

"We could wait until he goes home?" Simon suggested.

He was babbling now; it was a bad nervous habit.

"No, we don't have enough time", Freya said, shaking her head. "It has to be now."

They continued staring at the screen for about 5 minutes.

"Maybe we should go, Freya. Maybe this is not such a good idea. Do we even know…"

"Simon, be quiet." She held up a hand.

"Sorry", he mumbled, "I babble when I'm nervous. Shut up, Simon".

Freya attempted to distract him. "Where is he?"

Simon was amazed by her calmness; she didn't look nervous at all. Actually the opposite - he could see Freya's delight in breaking the rules, even if she pretended it was for the greater good.

He checked the screen again. "There's a car leaving the garage." Simon checked the licence plate. "It's his."

Freya withdrew her side arm.

"What are you doing?"

"We can't take any chances."

"Just use your ID."

"Trust me Simon." He didn't say anything else.

The car turned the corner and when it stopped at the traffic lights, she ran in front of it, weapon drawn.

"Get out of the vehicle", she said, banging on the front of the bonnet.

The driver hesitated for a few seconds but then obliged, leaving through his side door.

"Simon." She indicated to him to take over driving. Seeing Simon and Freya enter James's diplomatic car, Fatima started the engine of Simon's Toyota Corolla and came in behind.

As Freya entered the car from the passenger side, she holstered her weapon.

James Reynolds was livid when he recognised Freya.

"This is America. You can't come in here." He continued, "If you want to talk, go through the…."

Freya indicated to him to be quiet. "Now, James, if you want to make it home tonight, I expect you to answer my questions."

"I always knew you were a homicidal bitch, Freya. But not this, even you are not this…."

"This is your first warning, James."

"You are fucking crazy."

"Who in your government knew about the attack today?"

"Freya, you will never survive this, I will…"

"Is anyone giving material support to a cell here in the UK?"

"Fuck you, Freya."

"We don't have time for this."

She pulled out her weapon and put it to James's throat.

"Answer my questions."

"You wouldn't." He looked at her.

Simon replied, watching the whole spectacle in the passenger mirror, "She would."

There was a tense moment. James looked nervously from left to right. But he still didn't crack.

He said very coldly, "This is the end of you, Freya."

Freya tried a different approach.

"How is Jasmin, James?"

He was wide eyed with shock at the mention of her name.

"Does your wife know?"

He didn't say anything.

"I want to kiss your lips…"

Freya paused for dramatic effect.

"I want to feel your body."

"I won't betray my country," he said quietly.

"We have copies. It would be…"

"You think you can threaten me with that," he shot back angrily. "My wife knows." He paused, "Our marriage has been over for quite a while."

Freya was momentarily stumped. She hadn't expected this. But she quickly adopted a new strategy.

She said slowly, "But does your daughter know?"

James said very slowly and very coldly, "You fucking cunt."

She grabbed her phone, James tried to stop her and they momentarily struggled with it. Freya regained the upper hand and played the recording anyway. In it he could clearly be heard panting in ecstasy and yelling the name of another woman.

He shook his head, "You cunt, you absolute cunt."

"We have photos, messages."

"Stop, just stop".

He took a deep breath, realising that Freya was deadly serious about leaking the recording to his daughter.

"OK," he said, calming the situation down and taking a deep breath.

She withdrew her weapon.

"OK", he said again, steadying himself.

"I don't know much."

She didn't interrupt him; he still hesitated before telling them and was struggling to get the words out. He looked nervously behind him as though checking no one was listening and then looked back at Freya.

In the rear-view mirror Simon's silver Toyota Corolla was following them, driven by Fatima. Simon waved at her and she waved back. In the back of the car, Freya continued her interrogation.

"I know….," he began, "I know…," he breathed, "that the Knights of Christ were responsible for today's attack."

"We know that already." She paused. "Keep going."

"We know some of what they plan to do next." He paused. "If they are successful it will completely destroy us", he looked at her with terrified eyes, "but we have an even bigger problem, there are some powerful people supporting all of…" Suddenly there was a sound of something like fireworks. Simon tried to control the car but it veered from side to side.

Freya shouted, "Drive, drive."

The bullets came in from all directions; Freya ducked down as the window smashed, Simon began accelerating faster to escape the slugs. The front left-hand wheel blew out, sending the car into a spin. Simon pulled the steering wheel harder attempting to regain control but to no avail; they veered off course spiralling down a grassy bank.

The windows shattered; Freya, James and Simon were thrown

violently to one side as the car flew through the air. It came down in an unceremonious heap of tangled wreckage by the side of the road.

14:24

Prime Minister James

"I understand, Mr President."

He hung up the phone. In the room, listening to the conversation, were the NSC chief, the chief of the Defence Staff, Hill the Cabinet Secretary and a number of intelligence analysts.

Hill began, "He said point blank that their personnel won't be leaving."

The Prime Minister nodded deep in thought, he was deeply annoyed by Hill's 'I told you so' manner.

He turned to the Chief of the Defence Staff. "I want you to quietly draw up contingencies for the military to escort them out."

The Chief of the Defence Staff looked startled. "Prime Minister, don't you think that we can reach some kind of compromise? This could lead us to a very dark place, very quickly."

"It's a precaution, hopefully it doesn't come to that, but we need to show our resolve."

"What if they continue to refuse?"

"We need to show that we are in the position of power."

Hill began, "Prime Minister, we can extend the deadline. Reach some kind of compromise."

"No."

"But Prime Minister."

"No." He slammed his hand on the table. "I REFUSE to be bullied."

The assorted officials looked at each other with deep confusion and fright. What had happened to him? He had been a shell of a man only days earlier. The machinery of government now wanted the old pliable Prime Minister, the one they could effectively manage, not this new force of nature who was pushing their country into a diplomatic meltdown.

14:34

H

H stood in his office looking over the river Thames, the sun just above the horizon, its last rays filling the room. In the room were two members of the Special Forces Joint Liaison Task Force, Mohammed and Dmitry.

"Sir, the internal security officers can't find any trace of Freya, Simon or Fatima."

"Dammit." He continued, "But they have trackers?"

"Yes, Sir. But the range is limited, we would have to be within a few kilometres to pick up a signal."

"OK, go back to their last known position and retrace their steps. We must find them."

"Right away."

He saluted, beckoned to his companion, and then left.

H thought, where the hell are they?

15:00 to 16:00 PM

Freya

They heard a dull drone, the engine of some kind of motorised vehicle. The noise woke Freya slowly, lost between consciousness and unconsciousness. Burning aches and pains travelled up and down the length of her back. Everything was blurry, she couldn't tell which way was up, and her hands were bound with thick painful plastic ribbons. A cut in her arm was bleeding freely, caught by something metallic and sharp. She tried to cry out but the sound was muffled by a gag blocking her mouth.

She shifted her bodyweight to the left slightly, wanting to change her uncomfortable position. Using her elbows and knees she kicked up once and then fell back again. After several revolutions she was very slowly inching her way forwards. She came into contact with something hard and bone like. It was another body; she could feel its warmth and it was comforting to know that she wasn't alone and not the only one alive. She inched forward again in the vain hope that her movement would rouse the second presence, but nothing happened.

The car suddenly stopped and the doors opened. It was freezing and she missed the warmth of the vehicle, she struggled with her hands, trying to loosen the grip of the cable tie. She tried a technique she had learnt in the special forces during her evasion training. She gradually moved her wrists upwards and downwards. The idea was to gradually loosen the bonds over several hours; however, she soon realised that there was no give in them.

She wasn't panicking; MI5 had a tracker on them and they wouldn't be that difficult to find. She was sure that H would make it a priority to rescue them; whatever he thought about her she knew that deep down he cared for his people and would do everything he could to find them. She was frustrated that she had no idea how long she had been unconscious and therefore had no idea of how far they had travelled. Her training had taught her to build a memory walkway of the route she had travelled but she hadn't managed to do this. Mostly she was just annoyed; this was a waste of her time, she needed to get out of there and prevent the next attack.

After some time, she was lifted up and forced to walk in a straight line. A patch of light began to appear in her peripheral vision which she slowly realised was a window. Upon entering the room, she was placed in an uncomfortable chair and her blindfold was ripped off. She struggled to see for some moments as the light filled her vision, until she made out a dark shape, a tanned man with a beard, a white shirt and a woolly black hat. He had the slight trace of a Middle Eastern accent.

"Now tell me very quickly. What were you doing with James Reynolds?"

15:16

Prime Minister James

The Prime Minister entered the House of Commons through the side entrance and took a few moments to steady himself, psyching himself up. He was ready for the inquisition and would show no weakness to the blood-thirsty sharks.

Sarah had told him not to go. "There's little to gain, Sir, you have more than enough to deal with, deal with them tomorrow."

But he parroted Thatcher in saying "no," "no," "no," emulating her now famous formula. He felt he must confront the predators head on; if they even scented a hint of blood that would be his end. He strode up the stairs wanting to enter the atrium as soon as possible. He moved his arms like a boxer eager to get into the ring. This crisis had stirred something inside him that he barely knew he possessed. A wall of noise greeted him as he entered the chamber, cheers from his side and jeers from the opposition trying to drown them out. They rattled their order papers and stamped their feet trying to intimidate him, but he wouldn't give them the satisfaction.

He raised his arms to settle everyone down.

"Honourable members of the House." He directed his words towards the Speaker, who accepted them.

They fell silent.

"I want to pay tribute to Faisal, a dedicated public servant and friend of all of us here. He lived his life with dignity and sacrifice, he was a true servant of the people and he will never be forgotten."

The members fell silent as they remembered Faisal.

"I must inform the house that this is indeed a dark day. We now have clear evidence that our partner, ally and friend has been instrument in his horrific death."

He paused and raised his hands. "Therefore we MUST take swift action to confront this abuse of our sovereignty and show others that they CANNOT inflict great crimes upon this nation without consequences."

There were cheers as he said these words.

"Honourable members, I know that many will lament the action I have taken today."

"But bullies only react to strength." He paused. "And although this is tough action, this government also believes it is proportional to the crimes inflicted upon us."

15:42

Mohammed

Mohammed and Dmitry got out of their Range Rover and stepped into the road. The light was fading now, the shadows were lengthening across the street, dark pillars that engulfed the few waiting teenagers gathered at the corner, cigarettes in hand. The two MI5 officers scurried across the pavement, searching systematically with torches.

"Shit," Mohammed said.

They shook their heads and looked at each other; in his left hand was a phone, crumpled beyond recognition, the battery and sim card having been reduced to powder.

Dmitry said, "You'd better call H."

He dialled and H answered almost immediately. "Did you get her?"

"Just her phone."

H didn't reply, wondering what to do next.

"Try Simon."

"We already did, Sir, his phone has gone dead too."

There was an awkward pause; the two men were unsure what to do or to say.

"OK, we have footage of the car they left in. See if you can trace their movements using CCTV and any metadata you can dig up. I'm also sending you some witness statements from members of the public who saw the crash."

"Yes, Sir."

He put down the phone, he had tried to keep his voice calm but in his office H was furious. He knew that Freya was a brilliant agent but when this was all over he was determined to fire her. She always left a trail of devastation in her wake; he hated using assets to go out after her when they should be tracking terrorists. He smacked his hand again, releasing the pent-up frustration.

15:47

Trident41

It hadn't taken long for Trident to find a security flaw in Isaiah's coms system, one of his older zero-day hacks was still functioning and Isaiah seemed be using an older version of Android that was still vulnerable. However, there was a problem; he was using the app Signal for most of his communication which was almost impossible to crack unless you were the NSA.

However, he was able to take several screenshots using a tool that he had designed as a fun side project. He was very pleased that it worked, but he was only able to see partial messages and only while the app was open.

Trident kept searching for references to Brick Fish but he couldn't find any. However, he did find another phrase repeated.

"Red Sinai is coming."

Trident thought, what the hell is Red Sinai? He did a quick internet search for the words Red Sinai; there were several extremist Christian websites in which they talked about a Christian army fulfilling a prophecy of Moses, sweeping across the Sinai Peninsula in Egypt, bathing it in the blood of Muslims and reclaiming the country.

Why would Isaiah write the words Red Sinai repeatedly?

From his screenshots Trident couldn't read full messages. But there was something about a dam, a location, there was part of a concerned message from an operative about supplies of a number of chemical compounds.

Trident was smart; he looked at the location, the list of supplies asked for, looked back at the operative's message and connected the prophecy of Red Sinai. He sat back in his chair momentarily stunned and terrified, breathing heavily, shocked by the capacity of some human beings to inflict suffering on others and by the idea's audacity. He understood what Isaiah intended to do and it terrified him to the very core.

Isaiah wasn't going to change Egypt or NATO; he was going to destroy them both.

15:51

Freya

"Freya Caroline Mathews, Captain, 54824."

They hit her again and Freya tasted blood. The light was dim and it was cold, the room was tiny, too small for this many people. Its concrete sides were grey and unloved, crumpling under the weight of neglect. She couldn't see outside the window but Freya guessed they must still be in London.

"I'll ask you again. What were you doing with James Reynolds?"

"Fuck you."

This time they hit her in the stomach.

"Freya Caroline Mathews, Captain 5…."

Her chest started to quiver and she thought, bring it on, you fucks. That's right. She was psyching herself up, she had hours of interrogation training under her belt and she was psychologically ready. Freya knew that she just had to hold out for some time; she had to make it seem like they had extracted her cover story from her under duress. She also knew that the cavalry would arrive soon. Before leaving MI5 she had activated a transponder, concealed under a skin covered patch it was almost impossible to see even with a strip search. It had quite a good range of a few kilometres that could beat almost any signal blocker and was difficult to detect using standard bug detection equipment.

They hit her again.

Her sides burnt now; she did her best to refocus on her training. First you give only your serial number, rank and name. Try and build a relationship with your captors, they may take pity on you and make your treatment more tolerable. Her vision was blurry, deep shooting pains were travelling down her sides; she was getting tired but she was still resolute. "This isn't working," the big one said.

"Get the woman."

Two men appeared and opened the door, they were dragging in a body. At first she didn't recognise him or her, but after 30 seconds she realised it was Fatima, badly scared and bruised. Her left eye was bloodshot and there was blood flowing freely down her cheek. They must have tortured her first because she was Muslim, Freya thought, those sick fucks. The man pulled out a gun and put it to Fatima's head. She saw in those eyes a deep fear; they reflected a hundred emotions, pain, terror, resentment, shock. She couldn't look at them and she turned away.

"I'm going to count to 10."

He paused, "If you don't tell me who you are and why you were in the car."

He said slowly, "I will kill her."

"1"

He would do it, Freya was sure, there was no compassion behind those eyes. She leaned forward and pleaded, "Please don't, please don't do it," thick watery tears pouring down her face.

"2"

Fatima was terrified and screamed, "Freya, please."

He held up a small black box. "What is this?"

"I don't know what that is", she replied honestly.

"3"

Fatima began to speak, "We were here to….

"Shut up"

He put a gag into Fatima's mouth; she struggled with it and the towel only barely muffled the sound.

"4"

"Stop. Please stop," Freya yelled.

"Ok," she paused, "it's a transponder." She had no idea what it was.

"I don't believe you," he replied.

"5"

"For the love of God." She was desperate, "Please just stop, just stop counting. I told you what I know."

Fatima was rolling and shaking now, leaning forward to get away from the weapon, trying to escape on her knees. The other man grabbed her by the scruff of her neck.

"6"

Freya was thrashing, crying, desperate for them to stop. "We were there to apprehend James Reynolds."

"That's your cover story," he replied.

Fatima was screaming though her gag, yelling, the sound was sickening. Freya desperately wanted it to stop.

"7"

He held up the black box. "Tell us what this is."

"I told you, it's a transponder and they're coming to get us."

"Lies." The other man cocked the weapon.

She looked at them straight in the eyes and said coldly, while fighting with the restraints, "I'm going to kill you."

"8"

She stared into that face, hating everything about it, alternating between extreme pain and extreme hatred.

"I swear to god I will kill you."

"9"

"Tell us what it is, we trusted you and now you bring this."

"I already told you."

16:00 to 17:00 PM

President Leon

The President and Jane Sandai were having a walk and talk as he moved to a more secure location in a different part of the building. She couldn't understand why the President was wasting more political capital on this summit, she felt the agreement was dead and they should just cut their losses.

"Sir. we should leave; it would make a strong statement."

He shook his head. "I still think there's a chance we can resolve the situation."

"Sir, your deal is dead."

He looked away from where he was going, stopped, and looked at her with fierce eyes. "It's not over."

"Sir, you appointed me to tell you the truth when you needed it most."

He didn't interrupt.

She continued, "This summit is over and the British killed it."

"No."

He was refusing to accept reality; he began walking again and turned to her.

"No, we can still get those signatures."

"Even if you could, Sir, Congress..."

He interrupted her, "Don't talk to me about fucking Congress, they will realise how important this agreement is."

They entered another beautiful antechamber where they would spend the next few hours. The President sat back in the chair by the fire and Jane perched on the sofa, shaking her head.

He continued, "Get Hill on the phone; let's see if we can talk some sense into the Prime Minister."

Jane stood there speechless, unable to understand the President's intransigence. But feeling that she had done her duty, she didn't resist further. She called towards her aide, nodded towards Leon and then said nothing more.

16:04

Freya

He cocked the weapon, leaning over Fatima with a grin that showed that he got off on death and torture and hurting people.

"9"

"Stop."

They didn't say anything but stopped counting. "OK, I lied."

"We were interrogating James Reynolds…"

"10"

He discharged the weapon, there was a loud crack and Fatima fell to the floor, her blood splattering the opposite wall. She came to a rest on her side, as deep pulses of grief, anger, fear and pain pulverised Freya. It sent a spasm throughout her body and she uncoiled like a spring, she screeched and screamed again, kicking with every limb and her whole body rang with the noise.

"I swear to God I will kill you. I will kill you all..."

They shoved a gag back up her mouth, considered her for a moment and then slowly walked out of the room to have a cigarette. Freya rocked forwards and backwards on her chair with frantic energy, wanting to rip these evil men apart. Fatima lay on her side in a pool of her own blood, her eyes wide with shock. Never to love, never to feel, never to laugh - her vibrant life cut short in an instant.

16:08

Mohammed

Mohammed and Dmitry continued to follow Freya's last known direction when they picked up a signal. Very weak at first, it grew stronger as their car travelled at speed. The road was getting darker as they drove away from central London, the street lights becoming sparser, dilapidated Industrial estates and warehouses looming out of the darkness. The tracker was guiding them in the direction of East London but then suddenly died.

"Fuck."

"Check the equipment."

"It's dead."

"Shit."

"Check their last known position."

16:22

H

H's office was dark with only a small desktop lamp providing illumination, he stood in the centre of the room, nervously playing with his phone. He was on edge, unsure whether to make this call or not. Deciding in favour, he reached down and used an unusually shaped device with a cryptographic attachment. After a few rings the phone was answered but he was not the first to speak.

"Are we in the clear?"

"Yes. You're covered," H responded.

"I can't have this come back to me."

"Understood." He nodded.

"What do you want to do with the girl?"

"She must be stopped," he replied.

"Do you have a plan?"

"Yes."

"When will it happen?"

"Soon."

He had said what he needed to say in reassurance and hung up the phone. Outside the window the beautiful pale blue ribbon of the Thames was flowing freely. A few boats were drifting towards its banks, caught in the gusts blowing across its surface.

H sighed. A hard day was only going to get harder.

16:36

Freya

The men suddenly left the room. They looked increasingly unsettled and started looking around nervously as they left. Freya's body was tired, sagging like an old plastic bag, there was a nasty cut above her left eye that was bleeding profusely, the blood running down her cheek. She had a deep, sharp pain in her right side. She coughed again and her chest burned with every breath.

They were gone and, glad of the break, she focused on the words 'this will end'. She was physically, emotionally, psychologically exhausted. Fatima's death was an open festering wound, the trauma piercing her psyche. Minutes ago her body had been taken away and only the blood splatter remained. Freya stared at it for the longest time.

She wanted to kill them all.

Outside she heard footsteps and then a dull thud and a sharp metallic cranking sound as the door was forced open and two burly men entered the room. The left one rushed forward and grabbed her by both arms, while the other started cutting her restraints. They were extremely efficient and in less than 20 seconds they had sprung her loose. She tried to stand but fell back, struggling under her own weight. She tried to ask them who they were but her chest burnt; she struggled forward, determined not to be helpless, but it was too much. She needed both of them to keep her upright; she glanced around for the black box they had shown her earlier but she couldn't see it.

Mohammed and Dmitry now grabbed her from under the armpits and wheeled her out of the room. They seemed to be helping her so she didn't resist. Past the door the air was freezing and she shivered profusely, caught by the wind without protection. To her right, Simon was keeping watch outside. Seeing the huddled party, he left his lookout post and darted in behind them to shut the door. Freya almost tripped over a body lying in the doorway; he was placed diagonally face up, unconscious but alive, Freya thought. His body armour was gently rising in line with his breath. He was covered in mud, lying on his side with his arm spread out just underneath the nape of his neck. In the opposite building there was a ferocious argument going on; their garbled, agitated voices drifted across the car park. The pitch was rising and falling violently but the words were inaudible. Simon was sweating profusely, his whole body tense. He kept looking over his shoulder at the far away building. He urged us on, using his arms more forcefully.

They started moving in the wrong direction, "What are you doing? We have to get Fatima.. Fatima."

"Where is she?" Dmitry said looking extremely concerned.

"I don't know."

He whispered back, "I'm sorry, Freya, we can't. We'll come back for her."

"We have to get her," she said more loudly.

He put his finger over his lips. "Quiet."

"We'll come back for her," he whispered back.

"We have to," Freya started moving towards the building with the voices. The men made a swift decision, they grabbed Freya tightly and wheeled her towards the car. She had little strength to resist. They deposited Freya in the back seat of a black Land Rover and strapped her in.

She tried again. "We have to…"

Now Simon interrupted her. "Freya, we'll come back for her."

"No".

Freya stared, looking around. "Where is James?"

Simon shook his head; she knew what it meant.

"Fuck, he was our only lead." She let out a howl and hit the front seat. "Fuck, fuck." The car started moving.

Freya turned to Simon, full of compassion. "Are you OK?"

He nodded and said, "Fatima?"

Freya shook her head.

He fell back against the chair without saying anything; he also knew what it meant. Simon couldn't quite process it right now, but he knew it would hit him hard. They were all still in psychological shock from what had happened. Mohammed and Dmitry signalled to them to be quiet, their fingers over their lips, suddenly tense with fear. They could hear shouts now that were closer and the lights of a black Land Rover flashed in the darkness behind them. Freya didn't care, she started to cry, the immediacy of the loss washing over her in waves. She cried and cried and kept crying, great big tears that fell down into her lap.

16:41

Jericho

Jericho was back in his office after his meeting, confident that Trident was just about keeping it together but worried that he might not fully follow through. Right now, however, he had to deal with another crisis.

"They escaped."

"What! How?"

"Not sure."

"Shit."

"What about our asset? Is she still in place?"

"Yes, she just took delivery of the package."

"Good."

There was an awkward pause before the other speaker continued.

"I think we need a change in operations, I'll update you within the hour."

Jericho didn't reply.

"Also, Jericho, don't use this number again, move to the backup."

"Understood."

17:00 to 18:00 PM

1922 Committee

Just off Parliament Square, a huddled group of MPs hurried quickly towards their destination, their black coats wrapped around them tightly in a vain attempt to keep the cold at bay. They exchanged nervous glances to their left and right checking that the Prime Minister's informants hadn't followed them. They skirted the beams of the streetlight outside St Stephen's Tavern and were greeted by a rush of warm air. The interior was a welcome relief from the howling wind outside; this pub had been the haunt of many generations of politicians. Baldwin, Churchill and Macmillan had all drawn up their political visions here, determined to see a different, brighter future. These MPs were attracted by its grandeur and history, determined to see the back of a Prime Minister who in their eyes had lost his mind.

"We have to get rid of him."

They spoke in whispers in the corner of the room, scared to admit their treason, all of them were from different parties but were deeply concerned; the severity of the situation had bound them together.

"What he is doing is madness."

"I agree."

"We need to do this before any more damage is done."

They all looked scared and wrestled with this decision intensely, knowing what they needed to do but not sure if they had the strength in numbers to actually do it.

"How many MPs would we need to force a no confidence vote?

"48"

"Do you think we can get them today?"

He wrestled with his hair for a moment.

"Yes."

"As whip do you think we would win?"

He nodded, "It would be close but could be done."

As someone whose role was to keep order within the party, it was career dynamite to be meeting with the plotters. But for Archie some things transcended his immediate political interest. The future of the country was in jeopardy. All the usurpers looked at each other anxiously; neither of them wanted to be the first to jump but then one by one they all nodded.

"Let's do it."

17:12

Isaiah

Back at the compound Isaiah was raging, an anger spewing from the depths of his being. His hands were shaking, his fists were clenched, as they struggled to tell The Scorpion that his prize was lost.

"What do you mean they escaped?"

"They've gone."

Thick columns of condensation erupted from Isaiah's nose. His fury came out as a torrent of anguish that was terrifying to behold; his subordinates struggled to identify individual words in the cacophony of putrid anger.

He slowed down just enough for them to make out, "Get them back." He paused. "Now."

They picked up their weapons and assembled their backpacks as quickly as they could. Running to the cars that stood ready, once inside they revved the engines and began to follow the black Jaguar whose lights they could just make out ahead of them.

17:28

Freya

Faded pools of light shone through the car window as they raced past. Freya was slumped in the back seat of the car barely conscious; the ordeal had left her exhausted, physically and mentally bereft of adrenalin to sustain her. As she fell into unconsciousness she wanted to perceive nothing, see nothing and have a hot bath.

She was woken by frantic voices emanating from the front seat, their voices becoming more scared and agitated. She heard them again, "Are you sure?"

"Yeah, those cars are following us, the silver and red ones two cars back."

They started to sweat. He said, "Turn left, see if they follow us."

They continued left and the other cars followed them.

"Damn it."

"What do you want to do?"

Mohammed didn't say anything in response but began to speed up.

17:37

Trident41

Trident was walking briskly in the park; his discovery had made him terrified and he had felt trapped in the house. He knew that he had to call Jericho and convince him to put an end to this. He stood with the phone for a few minutes trying to make the call, raising the phone to his ear and back again before finally summoning enough courage.

"Look, we need to find Isaiah and put a stop to this."

Jericho didn't say anything.

"Where is he?"

"Really - I don't know."

"Call your asset at 5. Maybe they know?"

"Too risky."

"We should just let this play out."

"Jericho, listen. I joined Suez because I believed in what you were doing."

Jericho wasn't interested and didn't answer.

"But Isaiah's plan- it's far more than we imagined. If he's successful it will destroy the lives of millions."

He finally replied, "Trident, the best thing for you to do right now is run."

"Jericho, please... Red Sinai is..."

He put down the phone and Trident didn't get the chance to say *coming*. He stood there for a few moments temporarily stunned. He sat down on a park bench, wondering if he could simply run. No, his brain replied, you must do something, you can't simply watch this catastrophe unfold. Trident had tried talking some sense into them, but he now knew that Suez was over, diplomacy had failed and it was now time for direct action.

18:00 to 19:00 PM

Freya

Mohammed and Dmitry were getting increasingly nervous as a Vauxhall Astra and a Ford Focus began to gain on them. Dmitry picked up his phone and used his fingers to zoom in on their position. He pointed to a location on the screen, they exchanged a look of understanding and nodded, then stared straight forward, ready to proceed.

He turned around to them in the back seat and said, "Hold tight". Freya grabbed her seatbelt in two hands to tighten it and then held on to the handrail. She cradled her injured arm and moved it out of harm's way. Mohammed glanced in the rear-view mirror and gripped the steering wheel more tightly. He waited a few seconds and then revved the engine several times. When the lights turned green, they rushed across the intersection, veered right and braked hard. Their pursuers realised what was happening and tried to pass the outside lane of traffic, attempting to match them. They sped up a grassy verge attempting to cut off the corner but needed to veer right to avoid a number of benches. Behind them the other car was still in sight, only a few dozen cars behind them. In the right -hand front seat, Dmitri was giving directions.

"50 metres, turn left at the intersection."

The words were inaudible at intervals as Freya struggled to hear them over the sound of the engine. She could see them now in the rear-view mirror, four broad-chested men wearing civilian clothing. They looked extremely fit and it seemed that they might have one to one radios, as some of them kept tapping their ears.

She leaned back again and was violently thrown against the side of the car as they raced around another bend. Freya began to understand Mohammed and Dmitry's plan. They were trying to lose them in a series of one-way intersections. As they got closer, two lanes of traffic came from the other direction; the cars stopped forcefully just ahead of them as the lights changed. Accelerating past a crossing, they passed another intersection and then turned sharply into a dilapidated narrow alleyway. A series of non-descript white doors led into apartments on both sides and rubbish was strewn across the road. The entrance was obscured by two other buildings drawn tightly together. Mohammed and Dmitry both turned around to gaze out of the back windows, hoping that their assailants hadn't seen them make the turn. One of the pursuing cars came around the corner and then drove straight past the entrance. The passengers looked at each other and leant back in relief. Dmitry reported their position over the radio asking for back up and then paused for a few moments to let the adrenalin settle down.

The temporary peace was shattered by a rapid series of cracks that made the foursome jump; the slugs ricocheted against the armour plating terrifying its occupants. They couldn't see where it was coming from. Too scared to raise their heads, they instinctively reacted, stooping down low in the car to avoid the bullets.

Freya shouted, "Go now."

Mohammed put his foot to the ground again and the car began to move very slowly. A grinding, scraping metallic sound was coming from the car; Freya couldn't identity which part but there was something deeply wrong.

Mohammed shouted, "Shit, one of the tyres is gone."

Freya could smell the smoke now and continued to hear a grinding whirring noise, as the car struggled. Dmitry was now giving directions again, Freya held on as tightly as she could but she was slammed against her side. At the end of the alleyway, there was a high, solid, impassable brick wall; Simon and Freya glanced at each other with terror.

18:19

Isaiah

Isaiah was surrounded by pipes in every direction that spread out like an uncurled ball of string, one main trunk turning into many spindly threads, each of them with a destination. Below these, two men were working with a series of tools, attaching something black and metallic. There were a number of painted wooden boards to their left, chipped and cracked at the edges where they had been shaped to fit a particular space.

Isaiah asked, "Is everything in position?"

The Scorpion looked even more striking than usual in the evening light.

"Yes."

He squatted down to inspect their work, minutely peering at every detail for a few minutes, and didn't say anything.

He nodded and curtly said, "good."

He looked pleased and stood back up.

One of the men asked, "Are you sure about placing it next to the main valve? It will make dispersal slower and more diluted."

"Yes," he replied.

The two men looked at each other hesitantly but didn't challenge him on this point.

He spoke to them again, "Let me know when the other team is in place."

They nodded and he smiled.

He gripped his hands tightly and exclaimed, "This is our day, my friends."

They came together in tight hugs, showing each other their camaraderie and love in the most physical way possible. He looked both of them in the eyes and said, "Our children will grow up safe and happy in Christendom."

18:28

Prime Minister James

In Westminster the Prime Minister's allies rushed around Portcullis House trying desperately to piece together a plan to counteract what was happening. MPs walked up and down the corridors attending a series of informal open door meetings.

Sometime earlier the Prime Minister had been informed of a growing coup plot against him. He didn't like it, he felt like they could be struck at any moment, he wasn't a man who wanted to wait, if there was a challenge, he would always confront it head on.

There was a knock on the door, Sarah said, "Prime Minister, I have your daughter on the line."

He nodded and she passed him the phone.

"Hi love. How are you feeling?"

"I'm OK, Dad."

"That's good."

"But the men who came today, they won't let me leave."

The Prime Minister sighed. Not sure exactly how to tell his daughter about what was going on, he decided to leave out the details.

"It's only temporary, love; imagine it as a mini vacation."

"OK Dad." She continued, "But why won't they let me leave?"

"They just need to look after you right now, that's all."

"But they have cameras, who are they watching?"

As part of her condition she sometimes became fixated on certain things. This sometimes bordered on paranoia, but the Prime Minister had learnt over many years that the best thing to do was to distract her.

"What did you eat for dinner?"

His daughter's mood shifted abruptly; she loved talking about food.

"Lasagne, it was really tasty, filled with cheese and tomato and onion."

The Prime Minister couldn't see her but knew she was smiling broadly.

"That's good." He paused. "Call me anytime you want to speak."

"Of course, Dad."

"I have to go now."

"OK," she said painfully. The Prime Minister hated putting down the phone, guilt was already flooding his mind. But he was sure that he would have plenty of time to spend with her after all this was over. He passed the phone back to his secretary and tried to refocus on his work.

18:41

Freya

Dmitri pulled out his weapon and turned around. The vehicle had stopped and their pursuers had parked behind them.

"Fuck."

"It's not responding."

"What do you mean?"

"It's dead."

Mohammed hit the dashboard angrily and also pulled out his weapon. One of their attackers left the vehicle to take top cover and Freya lost sight of him.

"Shit."

She looked forward at her companions and then around again trying to keep track of their attackers. Freya tried to open the car door but Mohammed and Dmitry prevented her from leaving; she pulled the handle again but it wouldn't open.

"We're sitting ducks here; we have to take the fight to them."

Dimity replied, "We're safest in the car; they don't have anything that can penetrate it."

Freya shook her head, "They're going to hit us with technicals next."

The men in front weren't listening; they were on the radio trying to call for backup.

"Coms are down."

"Fuck."

Another man was approaching their vehicle now, taking cover on the right side of the alleyway.

"The police will be here soon."

Freya shouted, "Firearm response time outside central London is 20 to 30 minutes." No one could hear the next words because of the rasping of metal tracers strafing the vehicle and she shouted, "We need to take them before they flank us."

There was a brief pause while they reloaded.

"Fuck this," Freya said. "I'm not waiting here to die."

She leaned forward, grabbed a weapon from the weapons locker in the central panel of the car and undid the lock on the door. Mohammed and Dmitry started to implore her, "Wait Freya. What are you..."

She slid out of the vehicle, raised her side arm and began advancing on her first target.

18:52

Isaiah

In Wandsworth South a number of men gathered in a carpark; the youngest of these was nervous, he kept glancing left and right, jumping at any sudden movement. It was his first operation and he felt that he had much to prove to the older members of the party.

The most dangerous man in the room was James 'Abdullarhman' although he didn't use that name now. Upon converting to Christianity he had decided to jettison anything that might tie him to Arabs or Islamic culture. His code name in Egyptian secret police files was The Fox because he had a built a number of ingenious ways to escape detection. Aged thirty-six, he was married with two children and had quickly risen up through the Knights of Christ.

They pulled a number of armaments from a series of storage boxes, expertly checking every part of their weapons, looking for anything that might cause a jam. There was silence as every man in the group focused on the task of assembling their weapons. After a few minutes they nodded to the others in the circle indicating that they were ready to proceed. Lastly, they began to check each other's equipment in a series of procedures that Isaiah had taught them. When they had finished, they stood back and inspected their work. The younger men started to sweat and struggled to keep their breath under control, each feeling increasingly nervous. Finally, they checked their watches, packed away their weapons, left the room and drove out of the car park at different intervals of five minutes.

They were ready to unleash hell.

19:00 to 20:00 PM

Freya

It was freezing and her hands were turning numb against her weapon; she crouched down behind a low wall listening intently. She could hear shouts from across the alleyway and she tried to estimate their distance. She raised her head slightly, attempting to get a better look. A wide fan of automatic fire instantly destroyed the top of the wall that she was sheltered behind. Shards of masonry and dust littered the ground as Freya crouched back down, her heart racing. The voice of her drill sergeant was in her ear, stay still and you die. She was preparing herself to sprint to a different firing position on the other side of the alleyway when terror pulverised her stomach.

A young boy, who must have been about 10 years old, was just standing wide-eyed in front of the doorway watching the firefight. She tried to shuffle towards him but her legs wouldn't respond; every fibre of her being wanted to remain safe, sheltered behind the wall.

She signalled with her arms as best as she could and yelled at him, "Get down." He didn't move, he was just watching the unfolding devastation. Suddenly realising the danger, he panicked and tried to force his way back inside but the door was locked.

"Lie on the ground," Freya shouted at the top of her lungs. He wasn't listening, panicking, fighting with the door, as another wave of automatic fire fanned out across the wall and several bullets missed him by inches.

"Fuck. Fuck," Freya said to herself, angry at her own fear. She tried to move towards him again but a new barrage of tracers prevented her from doing so. She sat back down again, sweating profusely, and managed to shuffle a few paces, using the wall for cover. In a brief pause, she stood upright and dashed towards the door. She scooped up his small frame and made her way back into cover. The kid's breathing was laboured; he didn't say anything but lay still. She cradled his body as a series of sharp cracks destroyed the top of the brickwork. Freya knew that if they stayed there, they were going to die; she needed to get higher. To her right further down the alleyway there was an opening. She shuffled again along the wall keeping the boy as low as possible. She leaned over the wall, let off two rounds and tensed her body, ready to sprint towards the opening. But, as her body straightened, she heard a new noise.

Sirens.

Her heart leapt and she quickly ducked back down into cover. There was a rapid exchange of gunfire and men shouting. Immediate chaos ensued in the passageway, but she dared not look, just wrapped her arms around the kid and waited for it to stop. After another full minute there was silence. Being ultra-cautious as she went, she glanced over the top of the wall. One man was lying on the ground covered in blood and two others were lying on the floor, hands behind their backs.

Freya lay her gun on the ground and shouted, "Officer on duty. Don't shoot."

She then stood up very slowly, hands raised. Two men came forward, grabbed her and pushed her to the ground. They searched her vigorously for weapons and cuffed her hands behind her back. Freya looked around for the kid but couldn't see him.

"Show us your ID."

"Left trouser pocket," she replied.

One of the officers reached down and grabbed her purse; after a few moments they pulled out her ID. Staring down at the blank concrete, Freya didn't know what happened next, but one of the officers came back a minute later and said "seems ok." They let her back up and uncuffed her.

"I left my gun on the ground just there."

One of the other men went forward and grabbed an evidence bag; he put the firearm in the bag and then came back.

"Also there was a kid with me." She was concerned for his safety.

The officer said reassuringly, "He's OK, he's a witness and we've got him in the car."

Freya breathed a sigh of relief. "He's in shock. Make sure that he gets proper care."

The police officers looked angry, not liking what it implied or to be given orders, but they didn't respond.

The officer changed track and continued, "We'll need you to give a witness statement down at the station and we need to take this weapon as evidence."

"No."

"What?"

"I don't have time for that and I need my gun back."

Freya looked around. Simon, Mohammed and Dmitry were being led from their bullet-ridden Land Rover and ushered into the back of a police vehicle. An argument was starting as they resisted going with the police.

"Look, we are in the middle of a live operation; we need to get back to Thames House immediately."

"No can do, it's the law; we must now all submit ourselves to forensic evaluation and recorded witness statements need to be taken."

He was moving through his crime scene procedures.

"Let me speak to your commanding officer."

"She will say the same thing."

"Please get her."

He turned on his heel and a minute later his commanding officer came back.

"Is it her?" She indicated to the woman standing next to him.

He nodded, "Inspector?" Freya enquired.

"Detective Inspector," she replied coldly.

"We are in the middle of a live operation and cannot be delayed."

She nodded, "We appreciate that. However, my officer was correct, we must take you back to the station."

Freya said, "Call this number." It was H's number. "Why?" the CO said suspiciously.

"Just do it." Freya was tired, frustrated and angry.

She looked upset at her outburst but didn't reply. She got out her phone, dialled the number and came back a few minutes later.

"You're free to go, but we need to keep your firearm, we'll also need your clothes as evidence and we need to take a recorded statement from you now."

Freya waved it away and said with anger, "We don't have time for this."

"It will only take a minute," she replied.

"This is such bullshit." She said livid, but she quickly gave in, walked to the back of a patrol car and began undressing.

A minute later when she had finished, another officer came forward with a video camera to record their statement, a fresh set of clothes and the two captured men were bundled into a police vehicle.

19:18

Isaiah

On Nine Elms Lane parallel to the Thames, a Ford Transit van began speeding towards the American Embassy. It gained speed with every revolution of its wheels; a number of motorcycles on each side of the road had temporarily stopped the traffic, giving it a clear run. In the manner that climbers watch an avalanche as it heads towards them, the guards at the Embassy struggled to react and for some time just stared at the oncoming devastation.

They eventually raised the additional ram barrier that protected the guest entry point. The Marines and British soldiers guarding their posts opened fire on the truck but their shots had little impact, the Slugs ricocheting off the armour plating in a mushroom pattern. They failed to puncture any of the tyres and delay its advance. Panicking, the front layer of guards ran from their posts. The Ford Transit smashed headlong into the first barrier and tore it apart like tissue paper; it continued undisturbed for several metres before colliding with the secondary layer of reinforced steel. This tore off the right-hand wheel but its momentum still carried it forward. Finally hitting a bollard, it flipped over before stopping dead just outside the embassy's visa section.

Shards of glass littered the road and a small fire started in the petrol tank. Little of the vehicle was left intact, its windows had shattered and fuel was leaking on to the road. A shrill wailing sound began emanating from the Embassy. The second layer of Marines sprinted away quickly from the vehicle and some formerly inquisitive diplomats ran from the windows.

There was a moment of silence and then a deafening crushing sound that spread out in all directions. Fire exploded upwards from the bonnet and a shockwave emanated in all directions destroying everything in its path. It engulfed the front part of the embassy blowing out all the windows. Thick black smoke began billowing upwards through the

caved-in roof and the outside wall collapsed into the carpark, littering the area with masonry.

There was silence.

On the road outside, a few car alarms wailed and then the screaming began.

19:27

President Leon

A number of men came barging into the room, including the secret service chief who rushed forward and said, "Mr President, we need to go. Right now."

A number of staffers began packing up his papers that were left strewn across the room. It was clear a full evacuation was being undertaken.

President Leon didn't know what was happening. "What's going on?"

"There's been another attack, Sir. This time it was the embassy."

He looked deeply pained and concerned. "Oh my god. Any casualties?"

"We don't know, Sir, but it was a huge explosion. I'm surprised you didn't hear it."

Leon didn't move.

"Please, Sir, we need to go right now."

Everyone looked at him, as the President waited for a full 30 seconds before nodding. His staffers began packing again. He stood up abruptly and allowed himself to be escorted from the room; the corridor outside was in chaos. His staff were trying to gather up their things as quickly as they could, some rushing between half-open rooms. An aide carrying his suitcases came in behind him as he walked down the corridor.

His motorcade swiftly arrived for the short journey to Marine One in Hyde Park. The President had very little time to process what was happening before he was already in the sky.

19:39

Freya

Freya was just about managing to stand, upon returning to Thames House she had been escorted by several security officers to H's office. She didn't want to be there, but they wouldn't let her get back to work until she had seen him. This was a waste of her time and the more she waited the angrier she became.

She was exhausted, physically and emotionally overwhelmed by the day. But she didn't show it; she was determined not to show any weakness, not while there was any breath left in her body. Above her the white ceiling of H's office was illuminated by its mini chandelier, the dark shadows spreading out across the wall. Freya was furious, she wanted to scream, to shout, to kill. She was determined to find and exterminate every last one of the bastards who had killed Fatima. She barely heard the next words.

"You are immediately relieved from duty, pending an inquiry."

"What?"

She stared at him with so much anger that he was temporarily taken aback by the fierceness of her gaze, but he quickly regained his composure.

"You disobeyed a number of direct orders and Fatima's death..."

She became even more livid at the mention of Fatima's name. How dare he? Fatima was part of her team and she had supported her until the very end. She was her responsibility and now she was dead. She said the next words with venom.

"H, let me kill these bastards. For Fatima, in her memory."

He waved away the comment.

"We will avenge Fatima, but it won't be you."

She pleaded desperately and angrily.

"Look, H, you can't take me out of the field now." "No… No.." She pointed and exclaimed, each "No" becoming louder than the last.

"That's enough, Freya." He waved his hand.

She suddenly lost control, overwhelmed by a torrent of hate, anger, injustice and grief.

"You cold hearted bastard, ...fuck you…" She began swearing, unimaginable swear words that she could not control.

H said calmly but with venom, "Freya, get out of my office."

Freya was still uncontrollable and started moving towards him, hands outstretched. "I will never forgive you…"

"Security, restrain her!"

A number of men quickly moved from their positions at the door and grabbed her arms. She struggled against them but they were too strong, even though she was writhing against them, twisting and turning.

"You bastard…"

She was dragged unceremoniously from the office, still swearing and screaming. After she was gone, H took several deep breaths. He straightened his suit and then returned to his desk as though nothing had happened.

19:49

Prime Minister James

The American President was on the line and the PM was surrounded by his team of advisors; by now they had finalised the arrangements for the President's evacuation. At a number of military bases across the country a standoff was ensuing; some British military units had gathered outside several American military bases, including RAF Fairford, but these were the exception. Despite the mobilisation order, some brigades were being purposefully obstructive and taking their time. Other units were below full strength and still gathering their heavy equipment from different parts of the country.

"Understood, Mr President."

There was some more chatter.

"Now look here, many of our finest have died today; I will not be lectured about security."

The line went dead.

The PM looked at his advisors. Hill spoke first, "What are you going to do?"

The Prime Minister was annoyed by the comment but didn't say anything; he was thinking. He knew the Americans wouldn't evacuate willingly and had planned what he would do since before the announcement.

"OK, we need COBRA to meet again and we need to plan what we will do next; they are not going to leave quietly."

The advisors stood looking at the PM in disbelief, again Hill said, "Prime Minister, again I reiterate - there are many ways out of this crisis."

He ignored his advisor and continued beckoning Sarah towards him. "We also need to plan a press statement and to get control of the conversation before it gets out of hand."

"OK," he looked at his watch, "we have 20 minutes."

He clapped his hands, "Get to it."

The advisors looked at each other as though willing one of them to be the first to speak out against the PM's wishes. But no one pushed back and one by one they began to move, fulfilling the PM's orders.

19:54

Freya

Thames House didn't have any cells; instead they used secure interview rooms to house suspects while they were investigated. Freya was stuck in one of these spaces, unable to go home, but she hadn't been officially arrested. Instead, she had been ordered to wait for a debrief and they had locked the door. She was angry, she had done nothing wrong and this was a waste of her time. She tried to use the time productively and sleep, but she couldn't. She desperately needed to speak to someone outside of MI5; hearing a friendly voice, Freya felt, would help her plan what to do next, so she decided to call her mother.

The phone rang several times.

"Freya, this is a nice surprise. Are you going to be home soon?"

"I'm not sure, Mum."

"Freya, what happened?" Her mother could tell by her tone of voice that something was very wrong.

"I think I... I think I failed."

It was hard for her to say those words, but it was truly how she felt.

"Now listen, Freya, you are the strongest person I know."

Freya didn't reply.

"Does this have anything to do with what happened at the embassy? I saw it on the news, what an awful business."

Freya didn't reply.

"I know you feel responsible, love. But just think about what you can do now."

"Mum, you don't understand. I…"

She wanted to tell her everything but the words wouldn't come and at that moment the door suddenly opened.

It was Alexander.

"Mum, I have to go now."

"Yes, Freya, come home s…"

She hung up the call and asked Alexander, "What are you doing here?"

He smiled. "I'm here to break you out." He held up a piece of paper from the Cabinet Office rescinding her temporary incarceration. Freya stared at it in disbelief and asked, "What? Who authorised that?"

He shrugged to say he didn't know; she didn't say anything more but quickly hurried after Alexander before the circumstances changed. In the corridor, he looked her straight in the eyes and said, "Let's find those cunts," he paused, "for Fatima".

She smiled, nodded and said with conviction, "For Fatima."

19:56

1922 committee

There was a scrum of people in the corridor of Portcullis House; office staff struggled to move past them as they shuttled between meetings. A stack of serious-looking papers was knocked to the floor as two MPs collided, no one taking heed of anyone else in the corridor. Archie of the Whips office strode across the courtyard of the House of Commons with an air of seriousness. The rebels gathered in his small office in Portcullis House, where there wasn't enough space for everyone to sit so some were standing.

"He's going today."

"What's the plan?"

One of the junior ministers replied, "A vote of no confidence. We have the numbers."

"We could go with a censure motion?"

He continued, "No, no," shaking his head, "We don't wish to trigger a general election, we just need to get rid of him".

"What about the party chairman?"

Another MP answered, "He's on board."

Archie nodded.

"So Laura's going to take over then?"

All those present nodded.

"Is everyone here?"

The junior minister again spoke, "Yes, the word's been passed round; they are staying for this vote."

"When will it happen?"

"Within the hour."

20:00 to 21:00 PM

Jane

The house was dark except for the living room, where a few rays of light shone in through the window from the streetlight outside. Jane was watching Pointless on the television and enjoying her evening ritual. She loved trying to guess the answers of the contestants; it gave her some satisfaction that even with her advanced years she could still get many of the answers correct.

In the darkness, she hadn't noticed their alarm being tripped and a number of men clad in black advancing down the passageway. They quickly broke through the garden door using a series of specialist tools. They were so silent and methodical that none of the neighbours noticed, busying themselves with their evening entertainment. The men gathered at the back door for a few seconds, then employed a police ram to gain entry into the house. The door crumpled under the first blow but didn't come fully open, as some carefully placed security devices preventing it from doing so. They hit it again before Freya's mother realised what was happening.

She heard the crash, her brain barely registering what was happening.

The men hadn't announced their presence and Jane had no idea why the police might raid the house. She tried to stand up and escape through the front door but she was slow, she had no idea who or what they were and only caught one glance at them. She quickly decided that they weren't the police and she hurried more quickly, struggling with her hip. The assailants continued to assault the door but were now caught in the gap between the frame and the wall; lights were turning on in the opposite house as the neighbours heard the noise. Jane finally managed to make it across the room, hobbling as fast she could. She grabbed her phone from the hall table and dialled 999. The three men smashed the door again and the invaders rushed into the house. Jane was panicking; unsure what to do, she ambled towards the front door, trying to escape on to the street, but she was locked in. In her panic she had left her keys in her jacket and she was fighting with the door. She could hear the men behind her and she only had a few seconds to decide.

She moved back towards the living room and tried for the window. But she wasn't quick enough; she tried to open it but was pulled back by strong arms from behind. She struggled, resisting, fighting.

The man pointed his pistol directly at her head and said, "Stop that."

She gave up immediately, transfixed by the weapon in the man's hand and her body became still.

"Move."

In her pocket, her phone had connected with the emergency services.

20:18

Prime Minister James

The Prime Minister stood in front of a waiting bank of cameras. He tried to give the impression of being poised as the press conference began, but he was gradually being worn down by the relentless pressure. White flashes revealed dark shadows across his face that grew more and more opaque.

"Ladies and Gentlemen."

He paused.

"We have seen yet another horrific attack on our soil perpetrated by cowards who would stop at nothing to destroy our way of life."

He got angry.

"This aggression will not stand. And all those responsible WILL be brought to justice."

The tension died back again. Several bulbs flashed.

"Our hearts go out to those families who have lost loved ones today. Their sacrifice is not in vain."

"They died defending their country and the wider world."

"We will never forget."

He came off stage, removed his speech from the podium and stood for a few moments.

His senior advisor came rushing up to him breathless and red. "Prime Minister, I think we should go to the House."

The Prime Minister didn't interrupt.

"There's a vote, they want Laura. They're gathering now."

"That bitch," the Prime Minister said under his breath, very quietly.

He thought for a few moments. "Get the car. We're going to Parliament."

His advisor nodded and made the arrangements, signalling to some others to his left.

20:28

H

H was inconsolably angry that the Cabinet Office had side-lined him and gone over his head to reinstate Freya. He couldn't believe it when he had read the signed order and had called to check its authenticity. He was frantically calling Whitehall to make his feelings known and find out exactly who gave the order. He considered resigning immediately and thought, if those bastards think I can't make staffing decisions, then what is the point in me being here?

His authority had been seriously undermined and after today H would have to consider if he had enough left to continue running MI5. On this question he didn't have an answer but felt it was pretty borderline. He legally had to comply with the order but that didn't mean that she was completely off the leash. Her every move was being watched and he let it be known to anyone who would listen that there would be hell to pay when this was all over. For now, a compromise had been reached whereby Alexander became her Minder and Freya wasn't allowed any deep access to the system.

They sat in the conference room reviewing all the evidence, hoping that something would jump out at them. They were using a set of tools Freya had designed. It took geographical information, communication data, travel pattern analysis and mainframe data. It used AI, machine learning and pattern recognition to try to predict what suspects might do next. It was a well-designed and formidable tool but the issue was getting the quantitative inputs precise enough that it could spit out useful and actionable intelligence.

"Run it again."

He nodded.

The computer screen replied with 27 possibles.

Freya shook her head. "It's too many." She rubbed her eyes.

She shook herself again trying to get some energy back into her body.

Her head fell. "We have to narrow the target area."

Alexander fell back in his chair.

So far, nothing.

Freya was determined to keep working.

Whatever it took.

Her phone buzzed and she looked down at it. The screen was locked, so she inputted her pass code.

Then her whole world collapsed.

There was a photo.

Her mother's face was bloodied and bruised; her arms contorted behind her back.

Freya simply stared for a few moments, disbelieving what she could see, thinking it must be some kind of sick joke.

Underneath the photo was written:

YOU ARE OURS NOW

YOU DO WHAT WE SAY

OTHERWISE YOUR MOTHER DIES

PAINFULLY

TELL NOONE

WAIT FOR OUR MESSAGE

"Freya, are you OK?" Alexander looked concerned.

"What? Yes."

She looked again at the photo; they had included an object from the house to show its authenticity. Freya couldn't fully process what she was seeing, but she needed to leave immediately. Staggering over the chair, she made her way into the bathroom. Upon entering she forcefully vomited into the sink, sank to the floor and cried inside the cubicle.

She blamed herself. I brought this upon her, she wailed as she wiped away the tears. I'm so selfish. Her head fell, all the energy drained out of her; she felt totally overwhelmed.

Freya put her head in her arms and kept crying. I put her in danger. She was happy to put herself in harm's way but had never even considered that it might hurt anyone she loved so deeply.

She cursed to herself, "Arrrrrrrg."

Freya couldn't understand how this had happened. There was a robust system in place for protecting agent's loved ones, she had helped design it, but something had clearly gone terribly wrong.

What could she do?

Nothing.

A hundred horrible questions came rushing thick and fast. Why did they abduct her? What would they ask her to do? MI5 had a system for agents under duress but it was formed as part of negotiations and active field operations, there were no procedures for something like this. Unless she told them, they wouldn't know there was a number to call.

Could I tell them? she asked herself.

No.

They had access to her work phone, they had sent the encrypted message there.

Her fear suddenly turned into anger. She was going to kill them; she was going to kill every last one of them. The anger brought a rush of blood to her head and she temporarily felt dizzy. She dried her face.

Could I use a different phone?

No.

They must have me under surveillance.

• She finally concluded,

I must do whatever they ask. I have no choice.

20:38

Isaiah

Two men gathered in twilight outside a water treatment substation in the south east of London. They were extremely fit, with Middle Eastern complexions, and were completely focused on the task at hand. They looked nervously left and right, making sure they hadn't been followed. They moved forward silently, each checking the coast was clear before continuing, and stopped in front of a heavy-set gate locked with a giant padlock.

The shorter man stooped down and grabbed some bolt cutters from a black holdall. He quickly snapped off the lock and a rat scurried away into the darkness. The men moved slowly and carefully into the courtyard, handling their bags with care. At the foot of the station door, the ground was strewn with leaves that had turned to a pulp.

Now the taller man reached back into the black bag and produced an electronic device; he set to work attaching a red and black wire to the locking system. A few numbers filled the screen of the device and after a minute the door sprang open. They hurried inside, carefully closing the door behind them; water pipes spread out in every direction and there was the continuous sound of rushing water.

Using their phones, the men identified the main water pipe using a technical schematic; one of them reached into his coat and pulled out a black parcel. Both men looked nervously at this parcel, their foreboding increasing as they took off its protective cover. They gradually began binding it on to the water pipe, taking great care as they worked.

21:00 to 22:00 PM

Freya

Freya was scrolling through reams and reams of data. She wasn't really concentrating; she tried her best to focus on the task at hand but it was difficult.

She kept thinking, what can I do?

She couldn't bear to think about it, her mother trapped in a windowless room with barely enough air to breath. Trying with all her might to gulp down oxygen while a tight gag constricted her mouth. The images of helplessness cut deeply across Freya's psyche; she shook her head again, trying to disrupt the disturbing flow of thoughts. Until they called, she must work, she must put an end to this.

But what would they ask her to do?

A thousand horrible outcomes flooded into her mind. They would ask her to betray her country, or they would ask her to reveal sensitive information.

She would never do that.

But how could I resist them?

I could give them false information. But that could put my mother at risk.

Freya stood up; there was no chance she could get some productive work done. She came into the coffee room and attempted to make a cappuccino. Checking that no one was watching, she began sobbing again, the drops falling into her coffee cup.

The time is 21:27

Simon

Simon was confused.

He had run into Freya in the corridor and it was clear that Freya was very upset about something. Alexander had also come over to his terminal and mentioned it. They had both asked her what was up but she hadn't responded.

Something was wrong.

He strode towards H's office and knocked on the door.

A gruff voice barked back, "Enter."

"H, I need authorisation to monitor an encrypted phone. A highly sensitive one."

He didn't reply but indicated with his head to continue.

"I think something has happened to Freya."

"It's probably just stress."

He shook his head. "I think it's more than that, Sir."

"OK, take a look."

"Thank you, Sir."

The time is 21:35

H

The light shone in from the open window. It spread out across the room in a diagonal fan illuminating the chairs to the left and right. H stood by the window overlooking the Thames, his brow furrowed as he made the call.

The voice enquired, "Designator?"

He replied, "Alpha Lima Echo."

There was a muted dialling tone as his call was transferred. Someone on the other end spoke for a minute and H replied.

"Are you sure you want to implement SALUS now?"

There was more noise from the other end of the line.

"But you said." He was cut off by the other voice.

There was a pause and he listened.

"I'm not sure."

Finally, he capitulated.

"Understood, Sir."

He put down the phone and started to sweat. Taking some papers from the desk drawer, he put them inside a locked briefcase and prepared to leave the room.

The time is 21:46

Simon

Simon was waiting for the system to process the tap on Freya's phone and while he was unoccupied, he returned to his earlier task of tracing all the communication records of Isaiah. He quickly found that there was a smart phone interaction that had a very unusual communication pattern. It was being switched off at random and had very specialised firmware installed. The user was hiding their communication in a very sophisticated way - the software had disabled the automatic cell tower recognition on the phone. They were then encrypting the message, bouncing the communication off several cell towers before turning their phone back on again in a different location. The intention was to screw up the location data for an investigator and make it much harder to track the origin of the messages. You could still track the device fairly easily but getting any usable location data was extremely difficult. Intelligence agencies had designed a number of tools over the years to recover this data but there was a problem; while you could get the gist of the location it was very difficult to pinpoint it exactly.

Simon tried some of these tools and what he found worried him immensely; it took him some time to confirm but then he was sure. There were messages coming from within the vicinity of Thames House. He tried to find another explanation but he couldn't, the evidence led him to only one conclusion. Someone in the office was communicating with the terrorists.

The time is 21:53

Prime Minister James

In Portcullis House the Prime Minister's courtiers moved en masse through the winding corridors, lobbying MPs before the vote of no confidence. The Prime Minister himself was frantically glad-handing anyone he could; he knocked on doors, took photos with staff members, shook hands with family members. A crowd slowly built as he traversed the length of the building. As he was about to reach the final door on the corridor, a member of the security services that the Prime Minister didn't know gave him a phone solemnly. He covered the microphone and said, "It's Isaiah."

The PM's eyes widened and he just stared, "You're sure?"

The man nodded. The Prime Minister's heart leapt; this could be a great opportunity. If the terrorists wanted to speak, perhaps there was some way of negotiating a compromise or tracking their location. He had to keep them talking., The Prime Minister accepted the phone and looked around. He couldn't take this call here, so he beckoned to his immediate staff and they walked briskly to his constituency office. The office was small and had only a few chairs; the younger, less senior members of the entourage had to stand while the Prime Minister and the NSC sat round the table. He placed the phone in the centre and put it on speaker with some trepidation.

"Hello."

"Mr Prime Minister, thank you for taking my call."

"Who is this?"

He already knew who it was but the call was being traced and he needed to keep them on the phone as long as possible. The NSC indicated to the Prime Minister to keep talking.

Isaiah replied, "I have placed dimethyl mercury above several of the largest distribution hubs in London. If you attempt to find the mercury or put down the phone I will release it into the water supply."

The Prime Minister tried to speak but Isaiah continued.

"0.01 millilitres diluted is enough to kill 10,000 people."

The aides in the room looked at each other with terror and the Prime Minister began to breathe heavily.

"With whom am I speaking?"

He needed to keep him on the phone.

Isaiah ignored this and continued, "You have the Queen Elizabeth aircraft carrier docked in Gibraltar. You are to order this carrier to attack the NAMRU-3 American military base in Cairo."

"If you do not comply with these instructions, if you attempt to find the poison, if you attempt to contact the Americans or Egyptians, if you deviate from my orders..."

The PM interrupted him, "We can't just move military assets."

"We will release the poison."

The Prime Minister's normally unshakable demeanour lapsed for a second.

Isaiah continued, "You have twelve hours."

He put down the phone.

The PM immediately asked, "Did you get a trace?"

The NSC shook his head after consulting with an aide. "No, it wasn't long enough, the communication was bounced all around the world."

Other intelligence service aides were poring over their laptops to see if they could get some actionable intelligence from the recording.

He spoke again, "Prime Minister, there are hundreds of distribution hubs in central London alone, we can't search them all in twelve hours."

The Prime Minister didn't reply.

"He also said that he had placed several devices, meaning that if we get one we might not get the others."

The Prime Minister didn't reply.

The same spook who had passed the PM the phone now spoke, "Prime Minister, Thames House just called us; a package was delivered that contains photos of a device attached to a distribution hub and a vial of something that we haven't analysed yet."

The Prime Minister nodded and thought, they are serious.

There was a period of awkward silence as the PM considered what to do. It was common for there to be threats to public infrastructure and most were ignored, based on routine assessments. This was different; this could be catastrophic.

The Prime Minister said, "Thank you."

He didn't say anything more for a minute, deep in thought. The silence continued and everyone started to look agitated. James eventually said, "Give us the room."

The assorted staff filed out and, after a minute, just the NSC chief and Hill were left.

He asked, "How credible do you think this is?"

"Very, Prime Minister; they've proved highly adept at dodging every layer of security we have so far, attacked us twice and delivered something which is almost certainly the actual poison to Thames House."

He turned to Hill. "Can we close down the water system?"

There were shocked glances amongst the officials.

"Technically, yes."

"But it would cause disruption on an unimaginable scale."

"We would have to ship in bottled water to every house in greater London, that's almost 9 million people. The hospitals, transport network, the fire department and other public infrastructure might collapse under the pressure. We would have to purge the system to check for any contaminants. The economic damage would be unprecedented."

"Can we do it?"

"Yes." His eyebrows raised. "But it would take at least 6 months."

"You have one hour to make a report detailing the options."

He looked shocked at the suggestion, but didn't say anything more.

"What about searches? Can we inspect the whole system?"

"Yes, but not in the time we have; it's outside working hours, so we would have to get the day shift engineers out of bed. Also the terrorists said they would release the poison if we tried."

"OK, I want you to coordinate with the NSC, the Military and OFWAT."

"Search every pipe if you have to."

PART 3

The Finish

22:00 to 23:00 PM

H

In Thames House the corridors were filled with people: techs, translators, aides, liaisons and others rushing about the corridors planning the response to the impending crisis. Gold Command was struggling with the weight of tip-offs garnered from the Embassy attack. The ones from foreign governments were prioritised and a filter devised, but the raw intelligence was difficult to sift through quickly. Despite the lateness of the hour, no one had gone home. H walked up to Simon in the corridor.

"Simon, can I borrow you for a moment?"

Taken aback by the politeness of the request, Simon agreed and followed his boss into a soundproofed anteroom away from the masses in the corridor.

"It seems you were right."

"What?"

Simon was temporarily stunned by H's out of character acquiescence, not noticing the look on his face. H simply gave him a tablet.

"What do you make of it?"

He looked down at the scripting, "Wow, this is AES 256."

"I know."

"Virtually impossible to crack."

"A message was sent directly to Freya using this encryption at 8:29; unfortunately, we can't read it but we do have security camera footage of her face." In the footage Freya began to sweat and the colour drained away from her forehead; she looked as though she was going to be immediately sick. She sat for a few moments and then left the room heading directly for the bathroom. Simon didn't say anything and handed the tablet back.

H continued, "I think she's under duress."

He allowed this to sink in, but still Simon didn't say anything, unsure how to respond.

"Her mother has gone missing. Neighbours called the police an hour ago, saying that they heard some kind of break in."

Now Simon spoke for the first time, "What?"

"Police went to check, there's signs of a struggle and she's not there. The area is being cordoned off as we speak."

"Fuck." Simon said under his breath more quietly, "fuck," his breathing becoming more rapid. It was awful to think that their families might be threatened by the work they do here.

"I'm going to tell her that we know."

He began walking towards the door but H stopped him with his hand and shook his head, "No."

"What?" Simon said, suddenly becoming very angry.

H was very calm and stated, "The reason she hasn't told us already is because they must have threatened her mother's life if she spoke to anyone." He paused, "If we speak to her the terrorists will know that her mother's a compromised asset. They'll kill her immediately."

Simon started out of the door again and fired back, "She has a right to know, H."

"Stop, Simon. Think."

"H, if it was your family." Simon said, "you would want to know."

"Simon, stop. The best thing we can do now is to sit on this."

"I can't do that." Simon began to open the door, but H reached out to put his hand on the door and stopped him from leaving.

"Simon, look, they must be monitoring her somehow, we must find out how." He didn't reply.

"We can't do anything until we kill the surveillance."

Simon didn't respond for a moment and then said, "What? How?"

"I have no idea."

Suddenly all the politeness left him and he fired at Simon, "But you'd better find out," he continued, "and work out a way of getting a message to her."

22:04

Prime Minister James

In a House of Commons committee room, the bright ceiling lights shone down upon a series of ancient paintings that adorned the wall. In the centre of this, the chairman of the 1922 committee stood solemnly to announce the results of the vote. The chatter died down as he stepped forward.

"I can report as returning officer that 354 ballots were cast, there were no spoilt ballots and the vote in favour of Richard James remaining leader of the party was 178 votes and the vote against was 176 votes."

There was pandemonium in the committee room as supporters of the Prime Minister jeered their disloyal colleagues.

Sir Bradley Oakley had to shout over the noise, "I can therefore announce that the parliamentary party does have confidence in Richard James as leader of the party."

The cheering continued for some minutes as supporters of the PM stood up and cheered. The rebels left quickly, pushing others out of the way, hoping that the leadership might forget their treachery. As the congratulations poured in, the PM wasn't listening; he smiled and played the part but inside James was already plotting his revenge. He would have liked to stay and bask in the glow of victory, to enjoy the endorphins now flooding his system, to thank his supporters who had remained loyal. But after a few minutes, a junior defence minister took him to one side to tell him that there was another call from Isaiah. The PM was disappointed and his heart fell immediately. But as he was still the Prime Minister he once again had to take care of matters of state.

22:09

Freya

In Thames House, Freya was struggling to keep calm. She pretended to be working at her desk but she couldn't concentrate, she was battling with her own breath, she jumped every time her phone vibrated, terrified that it might be Isaiah's men.

She psyched herself up: You can survive this.

To control the torrent of anxious feelings she took in another breath of fresh air, willing the deep breathing to settle her nerves. Her phone vibrated again; scared to look, she immediately unlocked the screen and saw that she had received another message.

GO TO DOWNING STREET

WAIT FOR INSTRUCTIONS

There was another picture of her mother. Bloodied and bound. Freya couldn't bear to look at it. Her heart pined to get her back and to kill those murderous thugs for daring to touch her family. Suddenly her emotions swung in the other direction; she was unsure again, anxiety pulverising her mind. Should I tell someone?

She was an agent under duress and she knew what the procedure was. But those guidelines were designed for people who were on active field operations. No one would ID challenge her here in the office, so Freya knew they must be monitoring her somehow. The only way to fix this was to find out how.

How do they know my movements?

There were signal blockers all over the office, so electronic eavesdropping was almost impossible.

But somehow they knew.

I could tell Simon.

No. They would know.

How could I tell him without alerting them?

I could write it for him.

Could be too dangerous. If they know I am no longer an asset they could kill her.

Think, Freya. You are running out of time.

Do they have a mole?

But even if they did, he or she wouldn't be able to monitor me all the time.

She couldn't wait any longer.

She must go to Downing Street.

Make sure that their plan succeeded.

That was the only way to keep her mum safe.

She breathed in and began to head towards the exit.

23:00 to 0:00 AM

Prime Minister James

For the last hour the on-call engineers had been fanning out across London. They were using a series of devices to monitor any disturbances in the pipe infrastructure. To avoid a panic, they were told that there was a major leak in the system that needed a patch. So these call outs were disguised as routine maintenance. In the control centre, they were using a series of machine learning algorithms to monitor inflows and outflows, looking for any anomalies, but so far they hadn't detected anything. Teams from the Met were studying hours and hours of security footage hoping that they could catch the group or groups that had planted the devices. One tell-tale sign would be the sudden drop in footage from a camera or an unusual activity profile, but so far they had found nothing.

The Prime Minister was now back at Downing Street, sitting at his desk. Surrounding him was a substantial team of analysts and policy experts. His office hadn't been designed for this many people but in a panicky rush to take the call a more suitable location hadn't been found. The phone began to ring again and every eye in the room nervously darted towards it. The Prime Minister answered with trepidation.

Isaiah started, “Prime Minister. I think you must have felt that I was bluffing. We have been tracking your engineers.”

The PM interrupted, “What are you talking…”

Isaiah continued, “You now have eight hours to attack the base. If you do not comply, if you deviate from these instructions, if you attempt to contact the Americans…”

The Prime Minister tried to speak again but was cut off, “We will release the poison.” He then hung up the phone.

“Did you get it?” the Prime Minister asked.

The analyst shook his head, no one said anything and everyone in the room looked exhausted. The Prime Minister didn’t say anything for a full minute and then said, “Stop the sweeps.”

Hill replied, “But Prime Minister we might get lucky.”

“Hill, you heard me. Do what you can from the control centre.”

Looking deeply unhappy, he nodded and stood there, hoping for further instructions; when none came, he left the room. The PM pulled the Chief of the Defence Staff to one side.

“It’s time for plan B.”

The chief nodded and grabbed his phone ready to make the call.

23:09

Simon

The assorted teams from the NSC, MI5, the Special Forces Joint Task Force and Special Branch gathered around a large screen set up in the conference room. They were rubbing their eyes and jerking their heads to prevent any loss of concentration. Sarah, the PM’s aide, had been sent from Downing Street to monitor MI5’s progress and to act as a communication point. Most of the agencies involved in the investigation were based at Thames House but some of the decisions were being made by the Cabinet Office. Therefore, it was felt that a new line of communication needed to be established.

Simon was working methodically at his console when Sarah offered him a drink. "Coffee?"

Simon didn't reply, absorbed by the task at hand. "Simon?"

"What, sorry? Fine, thank you." Not really answering the question posed and clearly not liking the distraction. But he suddenly looked up, realising that he recognised the voice, and seeing Sarah he smiled broadly, stood up and hugged her immediately.

"It's so good to see you, what are you doing here?" he said, still smiling.

"The PM sent me to speed up communication between Thames House and the Cabinet Office."

"Wow! I'm really glad you are here," Simon said, beaming.

"It's great to see you too, Simon, how are you doing?"

"I would love to catch up, Sarah. I'm really busy with something right now, but we should chat over coffee soon."

Sarah nodded, understanding. "What are you working on?" She began looking over. "Perhaps I can help?"

"No thank you, Sarah. I really appreciate it but I'm OK."

Sarah didn't press it further; for a fleeting moment she looked concerned but then disappeared to a different workstation.

23:27

Isaiah

Isaiah put down the phone; he was happy. Warm feelings were rushing to his arms and legs in a surge of intoxicating energy. For months now he had visualised what it would feel like to have this power; it was almost overwhelming. He had the might of one of the most technologically advanced militaries in the world at his beck and call. He could make them do almost anything; he alone had the power to make or break them.

Daniel said, "What do you think they will do?"

"They will do exactly what I have asked."

"How can you be so sure?"

"They have no choice; they know what will happen if they defy me."

"But Isaiah, we could…"

"Daniel, do not worry, everything will proceed according to God's plan."

Daniel didn't reply.

"All we need to do is wait."

23:32

Prime Minister James

In Downing Street, the Prime Minister was still surrounded by a host of advisors. Papers were strewn across the desk and there was a general sense of chaos engulfing the department as plans were implemented to find the poison. Officials were agreeing common positions, working with a range of agencies to beef up the security response, and the MET's counter terror team had just arrived. The chief of the defence staff spoke first to the Prime Minister, separating himself for a few minutes from the general hive of activity in the room.

"We can begin moving the carrier into position; next time they call we can try to attempt to buy some more time."

The Prime Minister nodded.

He looked very tired as the chief of the defence staff grabbed his phone.

"OK, Admiral, begin preparations to move the carrier."

23:37

Freya

Freya looked down the alley adjacent to Downing Street; its old nineteenth century lamp posts enclosed it on either side, the footpath barely wide enough to walk across. The wind gusted through the passage, gently impacting the trees on the far side. She had managed to escape Thames House with a little computer help from Alexander and by stealing someone else's key card from their desk. She knew that this was a criminal offence but Freya couldn't give a shit right now, her thoughts were possessed by only one thing.

Why am I here?

She was getting cold, so she shifted her weight from one foot to the next in a desperate effort to keep warm. She didn't like it, she hated this waiting. Then her phone vibrated, with another message from the terrorists.

She read it and lost all her composure.

Arrrrg!!

I can't do that!!

She sat down, anxiety pulverising her insides. This was her punishment, she thought, this was Karma, her past misdeeds slowly destroying her present.

How did I let this happen?

She breathed again.

Think, Freya.

If Mum was going to live she had to do it.

Breathe.

Concentrate.

Focus on what you need to do.

Her phone slipped in her sweaty palms as she sent the message she knew she had to. She paused, terrified for a minute, but then began walking up to the gate of Downing Street.

0:00 to 1:00 AM

1922 committee

It was late at night and a number of rebel MPs gathered in the Red Lion just down the road from Parliament Square. They sat in a circle, a sorry bunch, downtrodden, heads crestfallen bending over their pints, commiserating their loss. The landlord had closed the door and wasn't accepting any more patrons.

"We failed."

They had gone for the jugular but had failed to strike a killer blow; no one spoke for some time and they returned to their pints of beer.

"You know I thought we had him."

"We can't let this stand."

There were nodding heads of agreement; another said with a clenched fist, "I want to rip that man out of his chair at Downing Street."

"The damage he is doing is incalculable"

Others nodded.

"This country needs the transatlantic alliance to remain strong."

He gestured with his hands and there were enthusiastic noises from around the table.

"Maybe it's time for a more direct approach."

There were inquisitive looks amongst the MPs in the circle.

"What do you mean?"

He sketched out a plan to the others at the table using a salt shaker, pepper pot and ketchup packet as props. By the end of the discussion the others in the circle were nodding.

One of them said, "When?"

"In a few hours."

00:09

Freya

Freya walked up to the security screen on Whitehall, at the entrance to Downing Street, its imposing gate rising high above her. There were two MET firearms officers in front and several members of the Armed forces.

She didn't have much time before the deadline and she really hoped this would work.

She walked briskly, as though she was an official late for an important meeting. She grasped her card and marched forward, clutching her black billowing coat in the wind, and waved the card quickly at the officers. But the gate didn't open, so she stood there completely still, unsure what to do or how to proceed; then they spoke to her.

"We have to call ahead, new security procedures."

"I'm very late," she said, harassed. "I need to go now."

He shook his head and held out a hand. "Wait."

She stood there nervous for a few minutes, breathing slowly to keep calm, but a torrent of nervous thoughts came to the surface. If she didn't get in what would happen to Mum? Would they see her as a liability? Decide she was no longer useful? She was terrified. She breathed again, steadying herself, but to her surprise after a minute or so the guard gestured to her to come forward.

She walked forward, unsure what to make of it but not waiting for them to change their minds. As she walked through the gate, she noticed a number of security changes. Bomb barriers had been installed in the road outside number 10 and the locks had been replaced. Military officers were now guarding each entrance in groups of four, their eyes twisting this way and that, clearly from the top of their rank. She tried not to look suspicious as she walked past them but they didn't give her much notice. She passed under the ornate black lamp posts that hemmed in the road, pleased to be protected from the howling wind.

She continued into Downing Street but hesitated for a moment; she couldn't just walk in through the front door of number 10. It was the middle of the night and she didn't want to be photographed by the semi-permanent press corps outside, all waiting for news on the current crisis. As she stopped, her feet naturally moved her in the direction of the security office at the right hand side of the main entrance. Pushing open the door with great effort, she made her way inside. The warmth of the office greeted her and it was comforting to be indoors again, with her objective now tantalisingly close.

The official simply said, "Name."

"Freya Caroline Mathews."

"Not here."

"Did they not clear me again? I have an urgent national security meeting."

She brandished her ID hoping it would convince her.

"No."

"It's urgent that I speak to Ben." Freya knew it was always good to name someone important when trying to enter a place; Ben was the head of the Joint Intelligence Committee and the most likely person to be in Downing Street.

"You're not on the list."

The official stared at her.

"This is a national security emergency; call him, he'll clear me."

"Sorry, if you're not on the list…"

She looked at her with a devastating gaze.

"No entry."

00:17

Simon

Simon kept scrolling through hundreds of data logs, fighting his exhaustion. He was left feeling deeply confused. Freya's tormentors must have a back door into the system, it was the only explanation. She had received something on her encrypted work phone, which shouldn't be possible. He also knew it would be much easier to breach the system firewall with a tiny data package, but unfortunately, it was like searching for the proverbial needle in a haystack of infinite size. He had tried the pre-designed software to find the patch but it hadn't detected anything unusual. He wanted to write his own software to do the job better but he didn't have time. So now he was down to checking bits of the system staring at lines of code. It was horribly inefficient but he couldn't think of another solution. He was tired and his eyes strained to keep focused; he had to find the system breach, only then could he help Freya, alert the Americans and save her mother.

Fuck me. I don't even know what I'm looking for, he thought, continuing down the lines of code, lines upon lines of script filtered through the codex. Compiled in more and more intricate layers, they found their way into different groups. Finally, after some time, Simon noticed something strange. He loved numbers and found beauty in them; to him they described reality more perfectly than any painting. He just had a sense when something was out of place, a quality that his tutor at Cambridge had noticed immediately. He realised that there was a piece of missing code in one of the final sequences.

The tiredness gone, Simon could see that this was the hack and he clicked for the ID on the software patch. A window appeared but the ID number box had been removed by the patcher. This was a very crude but effective way of covering your tracks if you didn't have much time. Whoever had done this had altered the structure of the system in a hurry. He opened Bombe trace, named after the famous code breaking machine at Bletchley Park during the 2nd World War; he hoped it could recover the deleted data. He ran the trace; it took a few seconds to retrieve a result. The ID patch came from within the firewall but there was still no name. Simon was disappointed, but pleased with his progress; he now knew for sure that they had a top tier mole.

00:28

H

H stood by the window.

"Are you sure, Sir?"

He paused and heard some more chatter.

"Everything is proceeding smoothly."

He nodded. "Yes, we have everything in position. Should be 4 hours."

"Has he been talking?"

There was more chatter on the other side of the line.

"Understood, Sir."

00:41

Freya

In the Downing Street security office, Freya was getting desperate, concerned for her mother's safety, and began arguing with the security woman.

"Look, I have important information relating to national security. If you do not let me in immediately, it will be your responsibility."

"Sorry. Not on the list. No entry."

"Call them." She paused. "Tell them Freya Caroline Mathews is waiting in the lobby."

"They won't clear it."

"For the love of God, please call them," Freya said desperately.

The officer looked at the phone, unsure whether to acquiesce to the request, and hesitated for a few moments. She clearly didn't like Freya and was enjoying the power she now had over her. Freya didn't try to push her again and tried a different approach.

"Sorry, I'm a bit stressed," she said kindly, "What's your name?"

The reply was, "Mary."

"Mary, I'm sorry, I'm sorry I was a bit forceful with you. It's been a long day. I really need to get to this meeting otherwise..." She indicated with her finger a slit across her throat, "My boss – well, he's a real bastard."

Mary nodded, seeming to understand about terrible bosses. "If you could pick up the phone and just call them I would really appreciate it."

Still unsure, Mary waited for 45 seconds and then signalled to another security official to watch her desk. She disappeared into a back room for a few minutes and then opened the door again.

"You've been cleared," she said very sternly.

"Thank you so much."

Mary buzzed the security gate and Freya began to walk up the stairs; at last it was time to do what she must.

00:52

Jane

Dark shadows spread across the room, accentuating every feature and fitting. Peering forward, Jane could only see the shape of the man's face in front of her, its features jagged in the light reflected from the window. She was in agony, the pain spreading upwards from her back into her neck and then down to her feet. It came in waves, rushing forwards at any instant that she tried to move.

The binds on her hands and arms cut into her skin painfully; she had lost the feeling in her left hand some time ago and she tried to wiggle it around in a vain attempt to get the blood flowing again. She desperately wanted to wipe her face; she had an itch just above her forehead that she was desperate to scratch. She tried to move in her chair again, attempting to make herself more comfortable, but to no avail. Her tormenter smiled broadly, watching her struggle, enjoying her suffering. She turned away again, trying to prepare for the next round of torture. They hadn't even asked her anything; it just seemed that this grotesque individual delighted in causing her as much pain as possible.

She was terrified at her situation, but she was also stoical. She was happy with her life; she didn't want it to end this way but if it did she felt pride in the way she had lived. She was proud of her family and her full life. Jane believed that everything happened for a reason and she knew that God would carry her away if the suffering was too much. She tried to focus on these positive thoughts and what Freya had said about being captured. If you are captured, try to build up a relationship with your captors, allow them to see you as human, and then they might give you some extra comfort.

At the time it had scared her deeply to think that Freya might be captured. She had said such things casually, not knowing the nightmares they would provoke in her mother, but now she was grateful for her advice. She still had no idea who they were; she heard them speaking a language she didn't understand - a bit like Arabic, she thought, but she didn't know. This must have something to do with Freya, but what, she had no idea. She waited silently, hoping, maybe if I am quiet they will leave me alone.

Jane thought desperately, All I want is to see a few more Christmases and to be there when Freya gets married. I will get out of here, she told herself, I want to live to see that.

She fortified herself again, you're not going to die here; they will find you sooner or later, just as the man turned back to her with a needle.

Jane started to plead and was suddenly terrified. "No, please don't. Please... no".

"What do you want to know?"

The man grinned broadly, clearly getting off on her terror, and brought the needle forward, looking for a vein. Jane started to struggle, and then to scream, shaking her restraints. The man slammed the gag more forcefully into her mouth and moved forward, methodically checking for the right place.

00.57

Freya

She reached the end of the corridor that led to the main series of offices adjacent to the Prime Minister's office.

The guard didn't even look as she approached.

"Name?"

"Freya Caroline Mathews. Ben will have approved me."

"You're not on the list."

"I know."

"Ben should have approved me."

He looked confused.

"Stay here. I'll go and check."

The other official stayed in front of the door to block her entrance.

He came back a minute later and said, "Cleared."

The security official relaxed a bit, checked her biometrics and face profile thoroughly against the card's picture. He then handed her card to a smaller official, who checked it a second time, running it through a scanner, and handed it back to her. She continued through the door, her heart hammering in her chest. She focused on her breathing, trying to stifle a surgc of adrenaline coursing through her.

She estimated that she had about 5 minutes to do what she needed to before they realised what had happened. She walked past the first set of double doors and crossed the corridor to the second doorway. As she approached the door to the main corridor she heard a scream,

"Halt, you halt."

Freya began to sprint down the corridor, dodging a grey-haired civil servant in the corridor, and she didn't hear clearly what they said next. As she turned the corner, she ran as fast as she could down the stairs attempting to escape through the door at the bottom.

They were very close behind.

1:00 to 2:00 AM

Simon

The server was gradually working its way through all the computations, struggling as it did so under the weight of all the number crunching. Simon drank some more coffee, jerked his head again and kept running through the lines of code. He was running out of time and he was angry; every attempt he had made to identify the mole was being thwarted. He desperately wanted to use the mainframe but there was no procedure or software to do so. Simon liked to be efficient and under normal circumstances he would have coded something to speed things up, but he didn't have time, so right now he was still having to do it manually. He wasn't sure how much to tell H; his stomach clenched painfully as he noticed several other anomalies where the system had been altered, but there didn't seem to be any pattern and he wasn't exactly sure what they were trying to hide. As he continued he felt increasingly frustrated. He looked and asked himself, who has the technical knowledge and inclination to do this much damage to the system? He felt very angry, who would betray us like this?

He checked the firewall diagnostics again; all the normal data recovery tools had failed. He wiped his brow and thought, Should I ask for help? He didn't want to alert the mole and he hadn't reviewed all the system damage yet. The more the tiredness crept in, the more he felt his ability to make rational decisions slip away from him.

1:11

Isaiah

Two men stood in the courtyard checking their instruments, surrounded by a mess of tangled pipes that spread out like an uncurled ball of string. They stooped under the lowest strand and came to a stop, being very careful with a dark shaped object about the size of a small egg box. They worked methodically for some time, shuddering profusely in the cold, connecting all the wires in a complex sequence and being careful not to disturb their precious cargo. Keeping their composure, they peered into the complicated electronic device in front of them, very carefully untangling the intricate set of wires that kept it in place. The second man's phone rang, so he carefully reached into his pocket and answered. He spoke in whispers and looked around nervously as he did so.

He spoke gently, "Yes, I've placed the second device."

The other voice spoke again and he nodded.

"No, we weren't followed."

More chatter.

"Good."

He quickly put down the phone and completed his work. The two men looked at each other for a few minutes, breathing in a sigh of relief as the tension was broken. They packed away their equipment, opened the outside door and quickly hurried into the night.

1:23

Prime Minister James

There was a knock on the door.

"What is it?" the Prime Minister said, annoyed, not liking to be disturbed.

Hill replied, "Prime Minister, I have the chief whip here to see you."

The PM nodded reluctantly, "OK, send him in."

Every fibre of James's being didn't want to deal with him right now; when he came it was never good news. But he resisted the temptation to send him away, as it could be important. The chief whip opened the door and came into the room. The PM was a bit too tired for pleasantries and said, "Martin, what's happening?"

"Prime Minister, I've just heard some more disturbing reports." He was sweating, having clearly run down the length of Downing Street.

"Members of the 1922 committee met again tonight."

The Prime Minister's interest suddenly jumped.

"We have sources who said that they met in the pub, but we don't know what they discussed."

"What do you think they plan to do?"

"I'm not sure."

"Do you think they will move against the leadership again?"

"I don't know, Prime Minister."

Tiredness got the better of him and he snapped.

"Well, what DO you know?"

He looked exasperated and didn't reply.

"Come back when you know more."

He didn't reply, quickly recovered his composure, nodded and left.

The Prime Minister sat back in his chair, breathing in the ramifications of this new development; he thought the vote of no confidence had been the end of it.

1:41

Freya

Freya was in handcuffs, she struggled against the restraints, attempting to release herself, but they were too tight. The Taser burn on her shoulder throbbed and there were shooting pains travelling up her back. She moved, trying to release the tension building in her neck, but it didn't help; anxious thoughts were now streaming through her unconscious.

Freya was terrified, the internal monologue spiralling out of control: what if they know that I failed?

How did they know to stop me?

They must know my mother is missing.

That was the only explanation.

But how did they know?

She couldn't explain how they had known to stop her, just after letting her through the door. H and Simon must have worked it out or this was the result of some kind of power struggle within Downing Street or miscommunication. It was very deeply confusing.

She was seething with anger.

I have to get out of here.

Knowing that every second she was trapped there was another second that her mother was at risk, Freya began grappling again with her restraints.

I have to get out of here.

2:00 to 3:00 AM

H

H stood in front of everyone, his torso upright, streaks of his silvery hair reflecting the light.

"You have one job today", he said defiantly while speaking to everyone in The Terminal. MI5's personnel were exhausted, only just kept together by passion for their work and coffee. Most of the techs were standing up in a vain attempt to keep themselves focused, but some had given up and were haphazardly slumped into surrounding chairs.

He pointed at them. "Turn everything on, call anyone in, use every single asset we have, let's do our jobs today and prevent a catastrophe."

While the assorted co-workers heard the words, they failed to lift the spirit of many. H lacked the intrinsic strength of leadership to really inspire people to follow him. To the assorted agents it felt like it was something he had heard in a film and was now regurgitating. It lacked real conviction. They would work hard to prevent this catastrophe, but not for him; they would do it to save innocent lives. Across the screens in The Terminal, streams of intelligence data were being processed and eliminated. Electronic communications were being assessed and distributed. Analysts were moving left and right, hurrying across the floor with tablets, coffee and paper. Simon was still staring at the system compiler, his eyes getting more and more tired as the hours went by. His vision was becoming blurry and he needed a mantra to stay awake.

Find the mole, find the bomb, save Freya.

He forced himself to look at the code again, wishing, wanting that special something to jump out at him. There was movement in the room and a ripple of excitement fanned out from the middle to the sides. He looked up as Alexander approached him and said, "We think we've found them."

2:29

Alexander

Alexander, Simon and H sat in an adjacent office from the main control centre.

"Let me show you what we found."

"We did an in-depth analysis of all the electronic communication patterns occurring across the city."

Alexander brought up a map on the main screen, where different coloured streams were moving in every direction. They were interacting with different nodes and then switching back again.

"We did an enhanced pattern analysis and found that some communication paired with the mobile phone network in unusual ways."

"They're using the 4G network?"

"Yes, and when we isolated these patterns we found they are synchronising the updates using the network, with devices that don't seem to be mobile phones."

"What?"

"How is that possible?"

"It's really quite clever." He smiled, admiring their tradecraft. "Not using a smartphone means that you avoid all our normal surveillance techniques."

"How are they communicating?"

"They're using washing machines."

"What?"

Alexander shook his head and suppressed a laugh.

"Yes," he said, almost laughing, "some of the more modern IoT appliances receive systems updates using the 4G or 5G network. So Isaiah has been using the system's updates to relay messages."

H looked at Alexander in disbelief and asked, "Can you track what they are saying?"

"We were able to get some of it but there's a lot of layers to sift through. We're almost certain it's them. He embedded his orders within layers of text contained within the system update."

H's demeanour suddenly changed; tell-tale signs of stress were dissipating, his eyes grew a little bit brighter, his back straightened.

"How far away are CO19?"

"9 minutes, Sir."

"Fully brief them when they arrive."

"Understood."

3:00 to 4:00 AM

1922 Committee

Portcullis House was silent, dark and eerie; only two MPs remained in their offices. Following the no confidence vote almost everyone had gone home. The more zealous had refused to concede defeat; they tried frantically to stir up more sympathy in other areas of the House and party. They managed to gain some momentum earlier in the evening but this had quickly petered out as more and more went home to sleep.

The first MP began, "There's not enough support for your plan; we can't do it."

He replied, "What, so that's it? We just give up?"

"I'm sorry, my friend, it's not going to happen tonight." The fight had left him and all he felt was an overwhelming desire to sleep.

"But keep the faith and we will get our chance again." He emphasised the word 'will'.

They didn't say anything for a few moments, then he began gathering up his papers and left the office, grabbing his coat.

"It's time to go home."

3:11

Simon

Simon was back at his desk and still wrestling with something that didn't make sense; he moved his mouse cursor carefully to avoid the edges of the box. He was becoming increasingly frustrated that his reconstruction process hadn't worked. Angry, he tried a new series of command lines.

Syntax error..11C

Bubbling anger was filling his chest. Why won't you work, you piece of shit?

He forced himself to calm down, trying not to let his frustration get the better of him. He was tired, he had been staring at the codex for too many hours. He got up from his workstation and decided to have a break. While he was carefully stirring his coffee it suddenly dawned on him. He could run a data recovery tool designed for system upgrades without affecting the main network. He was annoyed that he hadn't thought of it before. He came back to his workstation, the tiredness suddenly gone.

He first needed to test his theory without breaking the main network. The tool was designed to wipe the system and reinstall with factory settings, which could be a disaster if he got it wrong. He ran a virtual machine on his desktop, carefully compiled a system restore and then patched the codex. Very nervous, he moved his cursor towards the edge of the box and clicked *execute*. This time the computer was more congenial, finally responding with what he needed, and restored the missing data. Relieved, he tried the same process with the real system and nervously awaited the result for a few minutes. The deleted ID tag box came back and popped up on the screen. The name flashed on the screen.

He couldn't believe it.

It couldn't be right.

That's not possible.

Oh! Shit.

3:32

Freya

Freya heard noise in the corridor; unsure what to make of it, shuffling feet and murmured voices warned her of a group of people approaching. It was probably the police coming to take her into custody; she was surprised that it had taken this long.

What happened next surprised her beyond all expectations. The Prime Minister stood in the doorway, surrounded by a number of key advisors.

"Freya, what the hell are you doing here?"

Freya didn't reply; this was totally unexpected and she must use this to her advantage.

"When my staff told me what had happened. I couldn't believe it."

She replied, "I'm here to help you."

"How?" He looked intrigued.

"I think the terrorists have your daughter."

Hill spoke now. "Sir, I recommend you don't engage the prisoner."

James held up a hand to silence him. "What?" he said, shaking his head and getting angry. "Don't say such dreadful things." Freya could see the anger and terror in his eyes. "No," he said defiantly, "she's surrounded by security officers." But Freya could tell he was taking her seriously.

"There's a mole in MI5, the information we're getting is false."

Hill interjected again, "This woman cannot be trusted; she broke in..."

"Be quiet!!" James said sharply and continued, "No, you are mistaken".

Freya replied, "Call them now."

He disappeared back into the corridor; Freya couldn't hear the conversation. He came back a few minutes later looking terrified. He didn't say anything but his expression told the full story.

He accused her now, "MI5 told me that you are under duress."

"Sir, I swear on Lillian's life, as her good friend for so many years. Your daughter is in danger."

She paused.

"I am the only one who can help her."

3:32

Isaiah

Isaiah was watching Daniel intently as he spoke on the satellite phone; he nodded a few times and then closed the lid.

"Everything in place?"

"Yes, as soon as the planes are flying our people will begin their assault on the dam."

Isaiah nodded, "Good."

"How do you plan to transport the extra explosives?"

"The team is working on it."

He shook his head, "Isaiah, you know that without..."

He held up his hand, "We are working on it."

Daniel looked like he wanted to retort but decided against interjecting any more.

Isaiah continued, "Don't concern yourself with this, focus on the next stage."

They turned back to a series of black boxes with an assortment of cables, making sure that all the connections were tight and properly soldered.

4:00 to 5:00 AM

Jane

The room was cold and dark, illuminated only by a small pillar of light in one corner of it. Jane was tired, kept awake by the endless dull drone of the generator. She was exhausted, physically, mentally, emotionally. Pain cut right across her chest, she could taste blood in her mouth and she let her head roll back again. She didn't want the men to come back, but tried to focus on psyching herself up, engaging her captors in conversation. Trying to buy herself time, trying to get them to see her as human, but every time she had uttered anything, they had smacked her again.

She was furious with Freya; she was now sure this had something to do with her. How did I end up in this mess? Her spirit was fading, at first she was defiant, summing up stores of will not to show any fear or pain. Then she was compliant, hoping it wouldn't mean further pain; now she was numb, barely feeling the crushing blows or the humiliation. The door rattled open and her guard darted forward.

She tried to open her mouth, but before the sound came out her guard hit her forcefully in the stomach and she gasped. Intense pain shot right across her chest and back. The leader surveyed her with dark hawk-like eyes. His expression was resolute - not angry, not sad, just certain. He raised a hand, trying to prevent them hitting her again.

"Why…. , why… are you?" She could barely get the words out.

The man with the sharp eyebrows replied, "I don't enjoy this."

"Then why..."

"You are part of the system that crushes my people."

"Look, I have nothing..."

He hit her again hard, blood filled her mouth and she almost retched from it. Her head pounded and she was furious with herself for speaking.

"Your daughter betrayed us and this is her reckoning."

So it was Freya, that was why she was here. What did he mean? She betrayed us? Did that mean she was working with these murderous psychopaths? The idea was so awful that Jane could barely conceptualise it. She cried out into the night, wishing it to stop, to do anything, even die, to make the pain end.

4:11

Trident

In an act of desperation, Trident tried to call Jericho, imploring him to change course.

"We can't let Isaiah release the poison."

"Trident, you are looking at this the wrong way; this could be our final victory."

He gasped, barely believing what he was hearing; he was sure now that they had all completely lost their minds.

"What are you talking about?"

"Don't stand in our way," Jericho said menacingly.

Trident didn't say anything; it was clear that they were so possessed by the ends that they were capable of any means.

"No," Trident said and repeated, "No".

"Trident..."

"I want no part in this."

He hung up the phone.

4:18

Freya

Freya was still being kept in isolation in Downing Street but had been granted a laptop that she could work with. She busied herself with it, using what she knew about Isaiah and the Knights of Christ to help the Prime Minister's daughter.

She wanted more than anything to just sleep, just to switch off for a while, let someone else take charge. But her will and the vision of her mother being beaten and bloodied kept her fixated on the task at hand.

Freya kept coming back to something that she didn't understand. As she had walked into Downing Street she had passed several layers of security without being stopped. Someone within the Cabinet office and MI5 had kept approving her to continue. She didn't know who, but she needed to know. There were only two hours until the deadline.

4:26

Jericho

In his office, Jericho was having a serious conversation that he didn't want to be overheard. They had made a rule never to contact each other directly but Trident's defection had unnerved him.

He started, "I don't think this is a good idea."

The voice replied, "We need to make sure that the investigation proceeds the way we want it to."

"Yes, but you don't need to be in MI5 to do that."

"Trident is no longer cooperating."

"Yes, exactly; there's no telling what he might do."

"He won't do anything; he knows the consequences if he does."

"If you stay it will be very difficult to extract you if anything happens."

"I know."

There was a pause.

"It's OK; I have taken precautions."

More silence.

"I'm still not sure about this."

"Look, we need this; we are so close."

Jericho didn't reply and eventually acquiesced.

"OK, stay but be careful."

4:41

Simon

Simon was still in shock from his discovery; he couldn't believe it. He had to approach H but he wasn't sure how to; his legs were jelly and he could barely walk. If it was true, they were all really fucked. He knocked carefully on H's door.

"Enter."

He saw Simon and looked up from his papers. "Simon, what is it? I'm very busy."

"We have a mole, Sir."

These 5 words landed like daggers; H's body suddenly tightened and his breathing became more rapid. He dropped everything he was doing immediately.

"You have definitive proof?"

"Yes."

H indicated to Simon to continue without interrupting; Simon gestured with his arms. "I was searching through the database looking back over old intelligence archives when I found this."

He pulled out a tablet and showed H the Intelligence-indexing computer script.

"What am I looking at?" H replied.

Simon almost hung his head in shame that the Director General of MI5 couldn't recognise his own code. But he resisted the temptation and said, "This is the code used to store all the intelligence collected by field assets and the mainframe."

He paused, "It's been tampered with."

He let those words sink in for a moment.

"When you click here a box should appear detailing the files' edit times, software patches, upgrades, that kind of thing, but it's been deleted."

H was sceptical, "Could it be a system error?"

Simon shook his head. "I thought so too, so I checked; someone patched the system from inside the firewall."

The blood ran from H's face. "But that means..."

Simon finished the sentence for him. "Someone with high level system access altered system files on the main database."

H breathed out. "OK, call the techs and get them to do a full diagnostic."

"With respect, Sir, we don't have time."

"Look at this."

He pulled up the footage of Freya's warehouse raid.

H watched it for a few moments and very uncharacteristically said, "shit."

Simon pulled up the ID on the software patch.

H looked from the software patch to the warehouse raid footage, breathing heavily.

"She lied to us, all this time she's been lying to us."

5:00 to 6:00 AM

Freya

Following Simon's discovery, Freya had been quickly transferred from Downing Street to Thames House. She was handcuffed and escorted into the building flanked by three burly security officials. She requested that she be brought in through the back entrance, but H had vetoed this and had decided to publicly humiliate her.

Freya could feel the anger pulsating through her colleagues as she was marched through the foyer and into an interrogation room. She kept her head up, raised her chin and looked them straight in the eye, not submitting to their judgement. Inside, she vowed not to be ashamed and to clear her name. Someone started clapping as she was led up the stairs and another said "traitor" under their breath. Freya didn't rise to it and told herself that she would come through this. Turning a corner at the top of the stairs, they traversed the left wall, passing the photographs of former MI5 directors. She was led into a brightly-lit room with a two-way mirror, one where she had conducted multiple interrogations herself. They sat her down in an uncomfortable, spindly office chair.

H sat directly opposite her, flanked by Simon and Sarah. Freya was surprised to see Sarah there, although she knew why; the PM must be trying to keep tabs on how the investigation was progressing in MI5. H looked her straight in the eye and said, "Freya, you are going to tell us everything, from the beginning, full disclosure. Or you'll spend the rest of your life in jail."

He placed a witness statement in front of her.

"Is my mother safe?" She desperately wanted to know.

H sat for a moment awkwardly and eventually said, "We don't know where she is."

She pushed the statement away. "I'm not signing until I speak to her."

"Freya, grow up. We don't have time for this; millions of peoples' lives are at stake."

"I want to speak to her," Freya said stubbornly.

"We are working on it, but first you tell us everything, EVERYTHING you know and maybe we can stop this attack and find your mother."

Freya paused for a few seconds to consider the ramifications. They must know I am locked up by now. Would they kill her? No, her rational brain replied, they would keep her alive until they were sure that she was a burnt asset. What if they didn't? Either way, Freya mused, she couldn't sit by and let this attack happen; her mother would want her to do the right thing. She still didn't say anything and H tried a different approach.

"Look, Freya, if you give us some information we need, I will do everything within my power to see that you get a fair hearing."

She didn't say anything.

Simon said, "You cold hearted bitch. After everything..."

H growled, "Simon..."

Freya looked towards Simon, "It's not like that."

"Are you the mole?" he asked.

"No."

"You lied to us, Freya, to me you lied…"

"You don't understand."

H said, "Explain it to us."

She leant back in her chair but then eventually leaned forward, signed the document and began to speak.

5:24

Prime Minister James

In Downing Street, the tense atmosphere in the room was rising. Hill was red faced, unable to believe what he was hearing. Both parties were exhausted and tempers flared as tiredness got the better of them. Neither was in the best state to fully comprehend what they were proposing.

"Prime Minister, no." He stamped his foot in protest.

He looked terrified.

"I have no choice, Hill"

"Yes, Prime Minister. But we have no formal declaration of war," he said, raising his arms with anger, unable to comprehend what was going on.

"We have thirty-six minutes until the deadline," the Prime Minister said, reaching for the phone. "I have a duty to protect the lives of our citizens."

"Prime Minister. We have no guarantee that if we cede to their demands they will give us the location of the devices; they could attempt to activate them anyway."

He looked Hill directly in the eyes. "Hill, we have no choice."

"At least alert the Americans that we are under duress."

"Do you have a secure way to do this? A way you are sure can't be tracked by the terrorists?"

Hill looked to the NSC Director for support but none was forthcoming.

He shook his head. "They seem to have breached our communications and we have no idea how; it's a big risk."

They both looked at the Prime Minister again.

He said resolutely, "My mind is made up."

Barnard tried his last-ditch attempt to change his mind, "Prime Minister, you must not let your personal feelings cloud your judgement. Your daughter is ..."

The Prime Minister gave Hill a look that could have pierced armour and held up his finger.

"How dare you. How dare you, Hill," he said slowly, "If you were not absolutely essential I would relieve you immediately."

He didn't say anything for another minute, so angry he could barely speak, then he picked up the phone. "Admiral, bring the carrier within firing range."

"Yes, Sir."

"Is there an American response yet?"

"All Southern European forces are at a heightened state of readiness but no direct military response at present."

"Understood."

"Deploy when ready and do as little damage as possible. Do your best to make sure that there are no casualties."

"Yes, Sir."

He put down the phone; it was done, the advisors heard the conversation and hung their heads.

The Prime Minister thought, god help us all.

5:31

Freya

H and Simon sat across from Freya as she began to speak.

"I knew that we had a mole, or several moles, within MI5, all trying to manipulate the government into breaking ties with the Americans. They had tried unsuccessfully in several other influence campaigns to shift the political landscape in the direction of breaking our transatlantic alliance."

H and Simon didn't interrupt.

"They found themselves with a Prime Minister who was deeply sceptical of our partnership and who, following the death of his son, had a clear hatred for the US. They took their chance and have done everything they could to aid Isaiah and his band of murderous thugs to carry out today's atrocities."

Simon interrupted, "But Freya, you, the warehouse..."

Freya held up a hand and continued speaking.

"But what I didn't realise was the extent of the conspiracy."

She looked across the table. "Isn't that right, H?"

"What?" He looked confused.

"Throughout this crisis, you have done everything you could to bury the evidence."

"That's ridiculous. I saved you; I sent people after you."

"Yes, but only after others had found out that we were missing; you couldn't exactly refuse to go after us."

"Be quiet, Freya, you are trying to save your own skin."

"I was wondering who would have the power and resources to pull something like this off. It kept coming back to you; it was the only explanation."

Simon shot back, "But you blew up the warehouse destroying crucial evidence."

He showed her the CCTV of her running from the explosion.

"That evidence was there to frame you and me, Simon."

"What?"

"Yes. When this day was over, H was planning to find that evidence and be able to pin everything on us; luckily we got there first."

"This is crazy, be quiet, Freya."

"I thought so too, but then I did a bit more digging. You authorised my entrance into Downing Street."

"No I didn't. Stop this crap, Freya."

"But then I checked the system; for months now someone has been leaking classified information. The security system for our ministerial cars, our internal security procedures, my name and address: all of it came from you."

Simon got angry, "Freya, stop lying; you changed the system."

"Yes, I did, but only to find out who the mole was."

Alexander suddenly stepped through the door. H jumped in his seat and Sarah's eyes widened with shock. She sat rooted to the spot, unsure what to do, and looked around the room trying to gauge what was happening. Looking from H to Alexander to H again, Simon's facial expression changed from one of anger to confusion.

H shouted, "You can't come in here."

He said, "Quiet," withdrew his side arm and pointed it at H.

H was so shocked he could barely speak; Simon wasn't sure what to do as he looked between them. Alexander quickly unchained Freya and passed her a sidearm which she attached to her hip.

She asked him, "Did you get it?"

He nodded.

Alexander placed a computer in front of H and played the video; it was grainy footage of a helmet mounted camera in Iraq. It showed someone placing a roadside bomb just before a British convoy; H's voice could clearly be heard encouraging the squad.

"You organised this, didn't you? All those years ago you gave the order to go to that deadly street knowing that the convoy would hit a bomb and kill the Prime Minister's son."

"This is ridiculous."

"You even went so far as to tell the team with the Prime Minister's daughter to go to dark so that the PM would think she was in danger."

"Alexander, put down that weapon; what the hell are you doing?"

Simon looked at H and then at Freya.

"How did it start? How did Suez recruit you?"

H just said slowly, "Freya you are going to jail for a long time"

"Tell me where my mother is."

Simon saw that she was just maintaining control but she looked like she could strangle H.

"Freya, what are you talking about?"

She looked back at him. "Tell us, H. How did they contact you? What did they offer?"

He stayed silent, unsure of what to do next. Simon and Sarah both stared at each other, unsure of how to react to this turn of events.

H now smiled. "Everyone, let's calm down. There's been some kind of misunderstanding." He paused and said slowly, "That recording, it's a fake and all the other stuff I don't know anything about."

Freya said, "Give me your phone."

"No".

Alexander still had the gun pointed at him; H didn't move and he had instinctively raised his arms. Freya started forward to grab the device;

she reached inside his jacket, grabbed the phone and said to Simon, "Can you analyse this?"

Simon looked unsure. "Freya maybe... we… erm."

Freya looked at him with a fierce gaze. "Trust me, Simon."

H said, "Don't do it, Simon."

He said nothing and, looking more nervous, began connecting it to his laptop.

"Simon, this will be the end of you."

He opened his computer, hands shaking. "H, we have to check; if we find nothing then we release you."

He looked at Freya for reassurance.

"No. This son of a bitch gave them my address."

"Freya. He might ..."

"Simon, just do it."

He didn't say anything else and began downloading the contents of the phone.

5:17

Trident41

Trident was at his computer listening to heavy metal music; the angry lyrics helped him focus on what he needed to do. He tried for some time to see if he could disrupt what Isaiah was doing in London but he couldn't find an obvious way to do this.

Instead he turned his attention to what was happening in Egypt. He soon realised that some of Isaiah's operatives were still using older Samsung devices and luckily there were some pretty well-developed tools he could use to disrupt their communications. This might at least slow down their plans enough for the Egyptians to take them out.

Trident saw a new message posted on Signal which he looked at closely; it was a text file that he could screenshot more easily. It was an impact assessment of what would happen once Isaiah's operatives blew up the dam. It predicted that, following the explosion, only a few hundred litres of water would escape the blockage. Trident began to panic; this was much worse than he thought. It would completely bleed Egypt dry making the entire Northern part uninhabitable and starve 63 million people.

He sat back in his chair, thinking about how best to harm their network. He quickly launched a modified ransomware attack, hoping this would encrypt some key files and disrupt their communications for some time. Unfortunately, he rushed it and immediately upon pressing *execute* their defences kicked into action.

Trident yelled, "No…no."

He looked back at his computer, tried it again and studied the system. His attack had mostly failed although it might have encrypted some of the lower priority files.

Shit.

There was nothing more he could do; he couldn't stop it before the deadline.

He had only one option remaining.

5:27

Freya

They were still in the conference room and H hadn't been released. Alexander was still pointing his side arm at his chest while they studied his phone; no one had been allowed to leave.

Simon said, "Freya, there's nothing here."

Freya said, "No, there has to be."

He replied again, "There's nothing here, Freya, but... but that's weird", he said, noticing something on the phone.

"What's weird?" Freya suddenly sounded tense.

"Someone was piggybacking his phone to send messages."

"How do you know?"

He pointed at the screen. "Look, this should be the updated version of the app but whoever did this knew that the update patched a security flaw, so they've installed a command line here to prevent it updating."

He looked towards her. "Freya, he couldn't have done this."

"I told you..." H said and Freya replied, "quiet", while holding up a hand.

"Are you sure?"

"Yes, someone's been monitoring his phone and they used it to breach our network."

At that moment H's phone began to ring and everyone in the room looked at it. Alexander nodded towards Freya, "Put it on speaker," still holding his gun towards H's chest. Freya placed the phone on the table and accepted the call.

The voice said, "She's in the room with you."

Everyone looked from Sarah and back to Freya.

Freya replied, "Who is this?"

"She's in the room with you."

On the other end of the line Trident hung up the phone and sent Simon everything he had collected on the Knights of Christ.

Simon's phone began to buzz; he looked at it wide eyed and began scrolling through the content.

Sarah started to get up and Freya said, "Where are you going?"

Sarah replied smiling, "Bathroom".

Freya hesitated for a moment and Alexander moved his weapon towards her. "Give us your phone; once we've checked it you can leave."

"Freya, Simon, you can't surely think, after all our years working together."

"Sarah, hand your phone to Simon," she said menacingly.

She complied, "of course", turned around with her hand outstretched and as she did so tossed a flash bang grenade at Alexander's feet.

Freya reacted instinctively following years of military training and shouted "grenade", pushing Alexander to the floor. The device's magnesium core exploded in a shrill wail and period of intense light that filled every corner of the room. Sarah used the time to steal the key for the door and sprint into the corridor. She was already down the stairs before the occupants recovered from the shock.

"Everyone OK?" Freya said, coughing.

They didn't say anything but nodded, shell shocked but unharmed.

"Alexander, give me your radio." He passed her the radio and she ordered, "We need a full lockdown of the building."

No one replied on the other end.

She passed the radio to H.

"Tell them."

H picked up the radio. "This is H, implement Talon now and seal all the exits."

There was some crackling over the radio and by now Freya knew that the security personnel must have seen what happened on camera.

She looked at Alexander. "Let's go."

Both Freya and Alexander moved into the corridor with their guns drawn; she was suddenly wide awake again and enjoying another hunt.

She pointed, "Go that way; I'll continue down this corridor."

5:41

Captain Diamond

The carrier turned on its port axis towards the natural wind, straightened up and lowered ballast in order to stabilise her. The aircraft began to taxi on to the runways, their red, green and yellow lights reflected in the cockpits as they gently rolled across the deck. The shadows of the ship side crew fell across the runway and the dull growl of an engine starting up pierced the stillness of the morning. Within a few minutes, Brimstone and Pathfinder bombs were loaded on to the wings. Crews of men and women hurried about the deck connecting them to their launchers and hurriedly finished their final safety checks.

They were ready to launch.

6:00 to 7:00 AM

Freya

Freya was breathing heavily, holding her gun outstretched. She knew that Sarah was unlikely to be armed but that flash bang grenade had unnerved her and she wondered what other tricks she might have. She continued down the corridor, searching for any hiding places and called on the radio, "anything?"

Alexander replied, "Nothing; there's no sign of her."

There was pandemonium in the corridor as the MI5 staff left the building. Freya was furious; the Talon protocol must include an evacuation of the building for safety reasons. Everyone's passes would be checked before they left the building but it provided perfect cover for an escape. Her colleagues were rushing past her in every direction and she swore again under her breath, "fuck."

She burst through another door, gun drawn; a number of terrified techs raised their arms into the air. Freya simply said to them, "go".

She did a quick search of the room, checking the usual hiding places, cupboards, under the desk, but there was nothing.

Her radio crackled again, "Freya, we've got something."

She lost the signal. "Alexander." She said under her breath, "shit."

She tried the radio again, "Alexander."

"North East corridor, Level one."

Freya began to sprint, running as fast as she could; she ran past a number of frightened specialists in the corridor as she jumped down the stairs two steps at a time.

Her radio buzzed again, "Freya."

"Yes."

"It's not her."

"What do you mean?"

"It's not her."

Tiredness, exhaustion and anger got the better of her.

"Shit!! Start the sweep again."

Alexander didn't reply and she moved back up to her floor, vowing to have a serious chat with H about the building's security procedures following this episode. This was not the way to do a professional evacuation and was a complete clusterfuck. They spent the next 10 minutes searching the building with security but there was nothing.

She called Alexander again, "Anything?"

"No."

"Fuck, we've missed her. Fuck." Freya screamed in the corridor.

She knew that the communication delay with the guards meant they might not have known that Sarah was the target; she didn't have direct radio contact with them. They continued searching but every passing minute made it less likely that they would catch her.

"Meet me in the foyer." By now the search was effectively over.

She continued down the stairs and tried desperately again. "Anything?"

"Nothing." Alexander shook his head. Freya tried to calm down a bit and think about what to do next.

"OK, she can't have gone far."

She spoke to the security officers, "Contact the Met and put out a security alert for her in all the transport hubs in London."

Her phone was ringing again. Simon said, "Freya, you'd better get up here."

Freya began sprinting up the stairs, abandoning her search for Sarah; in another minute she was back in the interview room, where Simon was smiling broadly.

"This person, whoever they are, gave us everything. They even found a zero-day vulnerability in their system, only a few people in the..."

He was so excited that he could barely speak, rushing the words.

"Simon, what did you get?"

He said in triumph, "With this information and now that I know where the hack came from, I can use it to break their system."

Freya knew that he had taken the network breach as a personal insult and was clearly overjoyed to be able to get one up on the other side.

Freya looked around the room. "Where's H?"

"Not sure, think he…" Simon was momentarily stunned and lost his train of thought. Finally, he said excitedly, "Freya I'm in..."

In front of him were reams upon reams of data splashed on to the screen: locations, names of the personnel, operation data. Freya clapped her hands excitedly.

Simon looked at Freya and punched the air. "Freya we are going to pulverise these bastards."

Freya nodded and repeated softly, "for Fatima."

He replied, "for Fatima."

6:12

Captain Diamond

On the Bridge of the Elizabeth Aircraft carrier there was confusion.

"Check these orders again."

He handed a piece of paper to the bridge officer who quickly scuttled away, checking the coding on the transmission.

He came back and said solemnly, "It's confirmed, Sir."

The captain picked up the phone and called the MOD.

"Admiral, can you confirm the order?"

"Yes, captain, proceed as ordered."

He didn't say anything and put the phone down slowly. Unable to believe what he was being asked to do, the captain didn't move; he nervously meandered from side to side. He didn't say anything or execute the order, but remained deep in thought. Next followed a few awkward moments and the bridge crew started to look at him and each other nervously, unsure of what to do. Their normally decisive captain had completely changed temperament. After a few more seconds they again looked around the deck and still he said nothing. Finally, he signalled to his commander to follow him and they traversed the bridge in the direction of the captain's office. As they walked away the captain said, "Lieutenant Commander, you have the con."

He nodded and walked forward to occupy the captain's position on the deck. The crew looked increasingly nervous as the regulations of ship life were being undermined. The two men entered the office and the captain waited until the door was fully closed before he said anything. The two men stood opposite each other in his office surrounded by a number of beautifully framed photographs of ships. He paused before he spoke to Omar and then said slowly, "I've been ordered to attack the NAMRU-3 American military base in Cairo."

"What?" His commander's eyebrows rose into his hair; he was so shocked that he didn't say anything else.

The captain looked out of the window. "I knew something was up when they asked us to leave Gibraltar immediately."

"Captain, you can't give that order," he said resolutely.

He didn't say anything; he looked around at his ships and began musing to himself.

"To me this seems to be an illegal order. There's been no declaration of war; this is pre-emptive aggression against our strongest ally for no reason. It could potentially start a war with two countries and is deeply immoral."

"What are you going to do?"

He continued.

"Also with no permission from the Egyptians it will put our planes at serious risk."

The captain was a deeply religious man and took his oath seriously; he made up his mind.

"I can't follow it."

"This will be the end of you, Captain."

"I know, but no, no", he said, shaking his head. "No."

His second in command didn't say anything and the captain looked around his office and paused, glancing at the great ships that adorned its walls. "All my life I have just followed my orders and done my duty, but I can't. This time I can't."

He continued to shake his head; the two men looked into each other's eyes intently and Omar said, "I'll support you captain. Come hell or high water."

"Thank you, Omar. But this is my responsibility."

He turned towards the door again, swivelling on the axis of his feet. He strode back on to the bridge and stood before the bridge crew. The light from the landing strip streamed through the window, illuminating his face in an orange glow. He said slowly and deliberately, knowing what the words would mean for his life, for his career, for everything he had worked so hard to achieve.

"I'm about to commit a direct violation of our orders. I believe that they are illegal, immoral, tactically unsound and would start a war with two sovereign states. If there are any objections to this course of action, it will be noted in the log." He paused. "As captain I take full responsibility for this course of action."

He looked around the bridge; nobody spoke but, by this time, they all knew what they had been ordered to do.

There was silence for some moments before a voice cried out across the deck. "We are with you, Captain."

"To hell with our orders."

6:17

Freya

Following Simon's hack of Isaiah's computer network they had located the two poison locations and the terrorists' base of operations, all three of which had to be hit simultaneously. Freya was terrified for her mother and there was still no news of her. Freya prayed and prayed that they would keep her alive as she might be useful. She had insisted that she join the breaching team; Tariq the commanding officer was resistant at first but Freya had said fiercely that he could either kill her or add her to the team. Then she added that she had on the ground intelligence regarding the cell and that if it was his family what would he want? This finally convinced him and he gave way.

The briefing continued in earnest and the rest of CO19 surrounded Freya in the conference room. Considerable amounts of banter were exchanged, their faces erupting in broad grins. These were her guys and it was heart-warming to see them all again. Looking at the drone images, there didn't seem to be too many bodies guarding the poison and one location seemed to have been left completely unguarded, possibly to avoid attracting attention. The satellite coverage had thrown up a heat signature which was believed to be Freya's mother, shadowed by two men.

The plan was for the three teams to insert themselves, with one team using gas to incapacitate Isaiah and what was assumed to be his cell. The other team would use specialist bomb disposal equipment, checking for any booby traps, and the final team would rescue Freya's mother. Some planners had advocated the use of gas for the second structure but it was judged to be far too well ventilated for that to work effectively. Police cordons were being put in place and the deadline had already passed; they had to launch the assault soon. The OFWAT experts estimated that, if the poison was released, they could slow down its spread across the system by about 30 minutes by turning off the main distribution hubs. But there was little they could do about the pumping mechanisms for smaller local pipe networks as these were handled locally by a plethora of different water companies. Now that they knew where the poison was they had teams standing by checking for contaminants and waiting for clean-up.

They finished the briefing and Tariq said, "Good luck, everybody, and dismissed."

The teams picked up their gear, split into three different convoys and made their way to their target locations.

6:23

Isaiah

Daniel was standing over the monitor, nervously checking the screen. He was shaking his head and staring at the screen. "The planes are still on the carrier."

He added, "What do you want to do?"

Isaiah picked up his phone immediately and waited for a minute to be connected to the Prime Minister.

He said hurriedly, "This is your final warning. If those planes are not flying within 10 minutes, I will release the poison."

The PM was pleading with Isaiah, "Wait. We have a technical problem. Please give us some more time."

"No more delays. You have 10 minutes."

The PM said, "Wait, we..."

Isaiah hung up on him. He spoke to Daniel now.

"Get the teams ready."

Daniel nodded and began signalling to the men around him.

6:35

Freya

Three black vans sped past Seven Kings intersection; the roads were deserted and the convoy met little resistance as they approached their target buildings. No one spoke inside the van, each taking time to visualise the operation. The COs were unhappy; this was exactly the kind of operation they hated. Rushed, very little time to plan, complex, involving targets who didn't care if they lived or died and bearing a huge price of failure. Five minutes ago the police had confirmed that the cordon was in place and that the principals hadn't moved. There was still some debate about whether the raid would take place, with some in the Cabinet Officer arguing that they should drop a bomb on the locations. The MET was also less than happy that military personnel were being used on London's streets; they would have preferred using specialist police firearms units. Luckily, by the time the convoys arrived the bomb idea had mostly been put to bed, with experts arguing that it could leak poison into the water supply.

They left their cars and assembled their gear outside, where there was space to move. It was freezing cold and their breath froze as soon as it impacted the air. There had to be exact coordination between the three teams and they waited, struggling to keep warm while their communications officer confirmed that the other two teams were in position. Five minutes later the team had assembled their weapons and were just waiting for the green light. The communications officer raised his fist to show that the other teams were in position. The breaching team stood ready to execute, guns drawn. He began counting down silently with his hands and on zero they began running towards the first target building.

They crossed the open courtyard quickly and lined up against the back wall. The first man placed several breaching charges and the second began counting down. At zero the power was cut and the charges destroyed the door, sending it skyward. The men sprinted inside yelling "SAS" and tossed several stun grenades. One man raised a weapon and was immediately killed by a double tap from an MP5. The other man quickly surrendered and was dragged to the floor and handcuffed. The team secured the room, searching it extensively. They then set a security cordon and signalled to the MET forensics team that it was safe to enter. As the electricity came back, they were temporarily blinded through their night vision and most of the squad had to quickly surrender their scopes. Finally, they could see what the set up was; Freya came in, pulled up the masks and looked at the faces of both men.

"Shit. He's not here."

She said to the man on the right, who was still alive, "Where's my mother?", slapping him. He didn't respond, shocked by his sudden capture. Freya came forward to try and hit him again; Tariq grabbed her arm and said, "Freya, what the hell are you doing?"

Freya said angrily, "Get off me."

"Freya, they don't know anything."

"You don't know that."

He didn't reply but pointed towards the wall where a small explosive device was strapped to the water pipes. Abandoning the members of Isaiah's cell, Freya walked forward to inspect the tangle of wires attached to the pumping station. She looked at the explosives and the poison dispersal system and said, "Guys, this doesn't look right."

One of the men asked, "What do you mean?"

"I mean this looks like it was just assembled and is half finished. When Isaiah called he said he had already placed the devices hours ago."

The tech came forward and examined it. "Shit, is this an extra device?"

Freya shook her head, unsure what to make of it.

One of the SAS men let out a howl, "Fuck."

Freya was thinking and terrified. She spoke to the communications officer.

"Any news?"

He shook his head; she was desperate for her mother.

She spoke again to Tariq, "We have to take down the mobile phone network."

"What?"

"Look", she indicated to the tech. "This device is probably similar to the other one and there's a wireless transponder here; they are planning to detonate remotely using 4G."

"What if you're wrong?"

"Give me your radio."

He passed her the radio, "Listen to me very carefully; they're going to detonate remotely, we need to take down the phone network, it's our only chance."

"What?"

"Listen, just do it."

There was some static down the line and they came back.

"Who is this? What's your authorisation?"

"Listen to me. You have to..." She was cut off.

"Shit."

The techs were looking at each other, unsure what to do.

She asked again to the communications officer, "Any news?"

He shook his head. "We'll give you some as soon as they check in."

Freya turned back to the techs. "We'll have to diffuse the bomb manually."

The tech began unloading his tools and starting forward towards the device. Around her the SAS were finishing their crime scene procedures and collecting evidence.

"Tariq, get them to shut down the network."

"Freya, we can't just..."

She had stopped speaking, more concerned by the device in front of her. Metres away a police team soon arrived to begin forensics; they began trying to shuffle the soldiers away, tutting at how they were walking around, contaminating the scene. Freya and the tech began to work, carefully dissembling the casing of the device as they began to manipulate the right-hand bunch of wires; it suddenly sprang to life. Green lights swelled within it and spread out across the front panel.

The tech said surprised, "what?"

Freya didn't say anything and craned her neck to the back of the device. "Shit, it's begun to arm."

"What do we do?"

"What's the blast radius?"

The tech looked terrified; he had turned white and didn't reply.

Freya said forcefully, "concentrate." She said, jerking him awake, "What's the blast radius?"

He looked completely shell shocked, "I don't know - with this much semtex 100, maybe 200, metres. There would also be shrapnel discharge..."

Freya interrupted and shouted, "EVERYONE OUT NOW!!"

The assorted SAS members didn't wait to be told twice; they began packing up their equipment and began to run.

Dmitry tried to stay behind. "No. I'm staying with you."

Freya looked him in the eyes. "Go. Go now."

He was reluctant but started to move in the opposite direction.

Freya looked towards the Tech, "Go."

He looked terrified and was sweating, but he felt some obligation; he didn't know what to do and hesitated.

"It only makes sense for one of us to be here; you can give me instructions using the radio."

She repeated, “Go.”

The tech looked at her for the final time and then hurried away, leaving the toolbox. The wires spread out like a giant spider pinned to the wall, its legs criss-crossing in every direction. Freya was terrified as she fumbled and struggled with its tentacles.

Shit, there’s too many.

She breathed deeply, steadying her racing heart. She was not an explosives expert, but she continued, knowing how many lives were at stake. It was extremely fragile, the cords connecting the receiver to the main central container were frayed and had clearly been soldered in a hurry. She also couldn’t identify the power source, it seemed to be connected to a battery somehow but she couldn’t locate it. She took another deep breath and focused on finding the initiator.

There isn’t time.

She followed the wires with her fingers and guessed that it was probably inside the black central container. She carefully placed her screwdriver into the rivet on the top right hand corner screw of the lid, turning very slowly. She breathed deeply and waited, then kept turning, feeling a slight resistance in the webbing. Suddenly a switch slammed back, it clunked with a bracing metallic sound. The whole device shuddered, the spasm started in the middle and moved outwards like a shockwave. Petrified, she imagined fire exploding upwards from the ordinance and consuming her. Steadying a surge of adrenalin, she paused, took a moment to wipe away some sweat and tried to relax her shoulders.

Focus.

Letting her mind go blank again, she removed the lid and carefully placed it on the floor. She repositioned her torch in her mouth and used both hands to investigate the threads, trying to find the initiator. They were tangled and in some places she couldn’t tell which were connected to which. She loosened several clumps of wires with her hands and attempted to get her multi tool in underneath the main bunch. Finally, she found it, buried inside an inner black box connected to the main charge with a few multi-coloured strands. She put it aside for one moment and turned back to the rest of the IED, thinking about how to defuse it. Reaching into the tool bag she grabbed an ammeter and separated the wires into different chunks, methodically testing the power levels of each one and very carefully not disturbing the rest of the device.

Slowly.

She tried loosening the lid of the central black box containing the initiator, gradually feeling each wire to check for any give in it. She had to separate the initiator from the receiver somehow. She grabbed her torch checking the destination of a group of red wires, when something went wrong. Bright green lights erupted internally and the receiver turned on.

It was ticking.

She called on the radio, "I fucked up."

"What do I do?"

"What happened?"

"A countdown has started."

"Fuck."

"You have no choice."

"Cut the detonator wire."

"But what if it's rigged?"

The tech didn't reply but Freya knew what that meant. If it was rigged it would immediately discharge after losing power, killing everyone in the room. She looked at the detonator again; there was no countdown, it was improvised and could blow at any time anyway.

Sweating, she took a deep breath, reached forward and cut the detonator wire. Instantly the device lost power and Freya fell back in happy exhaustion, grateful to be alive.

She called over the radio, "Disabled."

She could hear cheers over the radio and she sat back for a few moments.

Then she heard another voice, "Freya, we have another heat signature heading towards you that slipped the cordon; stay there, we're coming to get you."

Freya immediately knew in her gut that it was Isaiah.

"Fuck", she replied, "Where is he?"

"Wait, Freya we're coming. Don't..."

Freya turned off her radio and drew her side arm; she took a quick glance at the drone imagery on her phone and began sprinting in Isaiah's direction. She passed a series of slimy pipes that led out into the mains, but she struggled to hear anything over the din of the rushing water. She knew what Isaiah was doing; he was going to poison the water manually. She continued to sprint towards the northeast corner of the pumping station; pipes and tendrils became ever more haphazard, crisscrossing above her in every direction. She peered around a corner carefully, checking that he wasn't there and then began running as fast as she could, glancing at her phone as she did so.

She was distracted by a noise to her right and saw reflected light for an instant. Before she could react, Isaiah had whirled around and let off two rounds which destroyed some of the masonry behind her. She raised her arms, crouched down and returned fire, but missed. He darted to his left and she followed close behind to the edge of a pumping barrel. She dared not look at her phone for his location, she kept her hands raised high and ready. She walked very cautiously, keeping her stance and felt carefully for her torch. The street lighting only provided the barest of illumination and she struggled to make out much in the dark. Breathing heavily, she sprang around a corner with her Glock outstretched in front of her but there was nothing. She crept forwards again, being as quiet as she could manage, scared that her breathing might give her away. She came to the next intersection and turned left on her axis. They suddenly collided into each other at point blank range, disbelief etched into both faces.

Freya lunged forward with her side arm but he knocked it out of her hand; he raised his gun towards her but she parried with her left hand, pushing it to the ground. He tried a right jab to her face which she dodged and she drove her right leg into the back of his shin. Isaiah swore loudly, turned around and grabbed her around the waist. She levered her elbows into the side of his temple just managing to get free; then they pulled apart again. A series of strokes followed which Freya systematically blocked one after the other. She attempted a scissor kick but misjudged the timing; Isaiah caught her leg and threw her over. She landed on the ground heavily, pain branching out right across her back. He reached down with his hands, grasping at her neck, and she gasped for air. The bind got tighter, she tried to break his hold, struggled for breath and was losing consciousness. She breathed haltingly and rasped, unable to escape, her arms flailing. She tried to kick free but to no avail as his body position now restrained most of her limbs.

Just before the final moment she managed to release her right arm, grabbing a small rock, which she slammed into his chest with as much strength as she could muster. He quickly fell to the ground but regrouped and tried to subdue her again. She hit him in the arm with less strength now. He came back on top of her again, using his superior strength to his advantage. Freya lashed out in a few furious strokes but to no avail - her strength had gone and she was almost out of the fight.

Jabbing pains spread across her torso and she staggered, winded. With one last surge of energy, she managed to lever herself with her left arm and raise her left leg hard into his groin. He staggered, hit by the intensity of the pain. Freya used the few free moments wisely; she side-stepped right, fell to the floor, grabbed his gun and pointed it at his chest.

"It's over."

He didn't move, just looked from the gun and back to Freya. He grabbed the small vial from his jacket pocket and began moving towards the water cylinder.

"Stop," she said, pointing the gun at him.

He shook his head and just kept moving towards the pumping arm, hands outstretched.

Freya cried, "Stop."

He didn't, and started to walk up the small ladder that ascended to the pump. Freya hesitated, failing to summon the courage. He climbed higher and began feeling in his jacket for the vial, so she let off one round that hit Isaiah in the leg.

He fell backwards from the ladder and let out a shriek of pain, landing hard on the floor. The water tank ruptured sending water spraying into his face. Isaiah coughed and spluttered as he ingested a significant quantity. Before he recovered his composure, Freya came forwards, yanked his arms back and handcuffed him to the ladder.

Isaiah said, "Freya.."

"Where's my mother?" She hit him hard across the face.

He said nothing.

"This is your final warning." Freya stepped back and pointed the gun at his head.

He didn't reply.

"Tell me. TELL ME!!"

She pistol-whipped him across the side of his face but still he said nothing and just held his head with one hand to stem the bleeding. The flow of water was gradually decreasing now as the tank emptied and Isaiah tried to break free of the handcuff. Freya came across him, preventing any shifts in body position.

Freya reached inside his jacket and grabbed his radio. "Call Daniel now."

He didn't do anything with the radio. Freya raised the gun again, "now."

He hesitated, then relented, finding it difficult to manipulate the radio in one hand. Finally, he changed the channel and tapped the radio saying, 'Brother."

There was no response.

He repeated, "Brother."

"Yes. Are you OK? Over."

Freya took the radio from Isaiah.

"Daniel, listen to me very carefully. If you don't release my mother to security forces within 5 minutes, I will kill Isaiah. Over."

There was static over the radio; she passed the radio to Isaiah.

"Tell him."

"Brother, thank you for everything, do as you have been ordered, we will meet again in Paradise."

Freya began to panic and thick droplets of sweat spread out across her forehead; her brain froze, unsure what to do. Over the radio she heard some static. She grabbed it back again from Isaiah and was just about to speak when she heard a single gunshot.

A piercing rupture spread out from her insides to her chest and back. Then hot billowing putrid anger overwhelmed her. She swiped forwards and punched Isaiah as hard as she could. He fell backwards unconscious, still chained to the ladder, his head slamming into the hard cold floor. Around her the rest of CO19 were arriving but she barely registered their presence. They picked up Isaiah and dragged him into a car. Freya was physically, emotionally, psychologically exhausted. She had nothing left to give. In the minutes that followed, she let herself be carried away by the medical team and into the back of an ambulance.

6:51

Prime Minister James

The PM and his staff were on the edge of their seats; the nervous energy still radiating throughout the room. They heard a triumphant voice cry over the radio, "Bonanza".

This was the call sign that Isaiah had been captured or killed and the poison had been neutralised. No one believed it; they were all looking around, waiting for others to be the first to react.

They heard it for a second time, "I say again - Bonanza".

The PM punched the air and said, "By God, we got him." The normally stoical committee room broke down into pandemonium as the NSC chairman punched the air and the head of the armed services stood up and said, "Good show everyone," smiling broadly. There were hugs, shaking of hands, clapping ringing through the air; all modesty was lost for those few golden minutes. In the middle of this cacophony, the PM's assistant came to give him a message. "I have H on the line."

"Yes," the PM said, indicating for the phone and sounding very agitated.

H started before the PM spoke, "Your daughter has been found alive and well."

The relief in the PM's voice was overwhelming. "I want to speak to her", he demanded.

H passed her the phone. "Daddy, hello."

"Are you OK, love?"

"Yes, these nice people gave me some breakfast, but they woke me up very early this morning; I was so tired, Daddy."

"One second, love."

He beckoned to Hill, who came forward hurriedly as the PM said, "Send an urgent dispatch to the Americans."

Hill nodded vigorously, understanding immediately.

He continued on the phone, "I'm glad you're safe."

"Are you going to come and see me?"

"Yes, love, of course. I have some work to do but then I'll come."

"OK, Daddy."

"Now, can you pass the phone back to the kind gentlemen?"

"OK."

She passed the phone back to H.

"Thank you, H. I will never forget this as long as I live."

"Thank you, Sir." He thought about mentioning Freya's contribution but decided against it, still smarting from when she had pointed a gun at his chest.

The PM asked, "How did you find her?"

"We apprehended a Suez agent within MI5."

The Prime Minister didn't reply and H continued,

"They had infiltrated our communication system and told the security team to go dark."

"Don't you have procedures for that?"

"When a team is told to go dark it means that any communication channel might be compromised. They are instructed to cut off all communication and immediately head to an off-the-grid safe house."

The PM didn't interrupt and H continued after an awkward silence, "In this case it took us some time to identify the safe house."

"H, thank you for what you did, but for the love of God you'd better update your procedures so this doesn't happen again. Understood?"

"Yes, Sir."

"Where did the breach come from?"

"Err..."

"Come on, man, just tell me."

H hesitated again.

"Sarah".

The PM almost dropped the phone in shock. "No … that. That... can't be right."

"She injured three of our officers and escaped custody."

"What? That's not Sarah."

H simply said, "I'm sorry, Sir."

"I've known her for years," he said, breathing in the ramifications. "How could she do this to us?"

His shock suddenly turned to anger. "H, you have to get her."

"We've got teams out there, but nothing yet."

James continued, "I'm going to sleep for a few hours, but I want an update as soon as I wake."

"Understood."

The time is 7.00 AM

Epilogue

Daniel

In the winding alleyways of Cairo's old town, Daniel had just finished a meeting with several leaders of the Knights of Christ. The communion had not yet elevated him to acting rector of the Knights but he was certain it was only a matter of time. Their plans had been delayed by Isaiah's capture but the explosives were being safely stored and moved on a regular basis to avoid capture. They still had coms issues but their operatives were gradually updating their phones, which was very slowly resolving the problem.

In a small huddle, they continued on their journey back to the main road, dodging the crowds and tradesmen pushing their wares. The overwhelming smell of incense, sweet tea and body odour wafted down the passageways. The party suddenly turned into a quieter alleyway, traversing a secondary square, and continued down another walkway with a series of flights of stairs.

Daniel heard the small pop of a rifle being discharged but had no time to react before the bullet slammed into the top of his chest. He tried to raise his pistol but was unable to respond before the second bullet destroyed his lower rib cage. Around him his security team were firing blindly, not knowing where it was coming from.

Daniel fell to the floor, his head to one side, his eyes beginning to darken. He tried to catch sight of his friends, but almost immediately fell into nothingness. Around him, his companions lay in pools of blood, staring up at the sky in shock. The street was quiet for a full minute and then National Security Officers from the Egyptian State Security Service rushed forward to collect the bodies before other Knights showed up. In the Office of the Egyptian President there were cries of triumph as the officers confirmed Daniel's death over the radio. They screamed with delight and hugged each other, forgetting the normal formality of the ministry. Someone began the chant of "Allah Akbar" and they all began echoing him, jumping to their feet.

Jericho and Sarah

Sarah and Jericho lay naked on the bed, basking in the afterglow of their lovemaking. After some time, Jericho sat up, lit a cigarette and grabbed his glass of wine from the bedside table. He walked on to the balcony, enjoying the morning sunshine; Sarah came to join him, slipping a hand around his waist. They looked out on the village, its shimmering green spires jutting up into the sky.

"Where should we go next?" he said, looking out towards the mountains.

Sarah immediately let go of Jericho and shook her head.

He continued, "Sarah, Suez is over; we need to go and live out our lives somewhere."

Again Sarah shook her head and replied,

"We made mistakes; trusting Trident for one, but this is far from over."

"Look, we had a great triumph; we damaged the relationship almost beyond repair."

Sarah shook her head, "It's not enough, they will soon rebuild."

Jericho didn't say anything for some time, smoking his cigarette; he tried a different tactic and carried on looking outwards towards the winding river some miles away.

"Sarah, Luke is gone and destroying yourself won't bring him back."

She said fiercely, "They killed him."

"Even the Prime Minister…"

"That's enough," Sarah said angrily, waving her arms as she began to leave the balcony.

"Where are you going?"

She grabbed her phone from the table.

"I've got someone I need to call."

Trident41

In an airport departure lounge, Trident was waiting for a flight. He hated travelling but he knew that it was critical to keep moving if he was to escape the authorities. Luckily one of his aliases was still undiscovered and those accounts hadn't been frozen yet, so at least he could travel first. He turned back to his beer in the lounge, reading his police file case notes and smiling. It seemed that all was not well in the investigation into his case; there were a number of frantic emails from the investigating officer about the lack of leads. Trident was glad Simon had steered clear of the investigation; he was sure that he could have found him with a few days of work but for whatever reason had decided that he had other priorities.

To take a break and pass the time, Trident started to play one of his favourite online games. He was just in the middle of a kill streak when the game froze; he tried to refresh his browser but it wouldn't respond. Worried now, he was about to disable his wireless network card and clean the browser when something happened that took him by complete surprise.

Superimposed on top of the game, a box appeared saying, *don't leave this page.*

Trident was scared, what the hell is going on?

Again he was about to close down his computer to stop their access and probable trace of his location.

The box refilled again, *we don't know where you are please stay on this page.*

Trident didn't move but his fingers hovered over the keyboard. He thought it was unlikely that they knew his real identity as he had gone to great lengths to keep it secret. They probably only knew him by his online reputation but the irrational part of him wanted to immediately destroy his computer. He hesitated, quite interested in what they might have to say; these were clearly serious people and what they had just accomplished was extremely difficult.

Exposure would like you to join our community.

He had heard of Exposure before, famous for taking on Isis, the Chinese government and finding paedophiles. They believed that they hacked for the greater good and often launched DOS attacks on arms companies.

To discuss further please create an anonymous account with Makeshift and send a message to gitspace164.

The box disappeared and then refilled again.

You have 24 hours

Trident sat there for a few minutes; he didn't want to expose himself to any more risk. But maybe this was an opportunity to use his skills for good. It might be too dangerous, he should wait for things to die down a bit, but then he might not get another chance. Maybe, he thought, I could join but choose very carefully which attacks I take part in and participate in those that I feel are meaningful. He sat there for some time, unsure what to do, but then eventually typed his answer.

Freya

It was a dull day; light rain gradually christened the adjoining headstones of the churchyard. Jane hadn't been particularly religious, but it would have felt wrong to have held the ceremony anywhere else. Members of her generation wanted to be laid to rest where they grew up, where they felt at peace, surrounded by their countrymen and in an Anglican churchyard. It was something deeply cultural and her family were determined to respect her wishes. For Freya it was too hard to be involved in the preparation, so her sister had mostly taken charge. It was a simple ceremony; Jane wouldn't have wanted anything extravagant. There weren't many people; she had been completely devoted to her family and little else.

The priest stood in the middle of the churchyard, presiding over a group of mourners all with their heads bowed. There were a few work colleagues, assorted friends from the home of her childhood and, of course, family. After the priest had finished, the small procession of well-wishers came to her coffin to say goodbye, all gently touching it as they moved past. Freya was in the middle of this, tears streaming down her face, too angry to speak.

Thankfully, there hadn't been too many questions from those present as to how she had died; an inquiry had been launched and Freya wasn't able to say anything until the coroner's report was made public. In some ways that helped; it would have made the whole occasion awful beyond words if she had to relive that dreadful day with every new person. As the coffin was lowered into the earth, Freya veered between sadness and hot boiling anger; she couldn't wait for the whole thing to be over. Finally, after what seemed an age, the mourners filtered away from the churchyard and she could be on her own. She didn't want to speak to anyone or discuss anything or hear how sorry people felt. She was livid in the depths of her being, she wanted to run from it all. She came around the corner of the chapel back into the graveyard, thankful to finally be away from the crowd, and screamed into the sky with all the rage she could muster. Freya vowed that she was going to find who did this, she was going to find them and kill them; she would spend every hour of every day if need be. She pledged, in increasing desperation, to those who destroy innocent lives in the dark, I am coming for you.

THANK YOU FOR READING

If you enjoyed this it would be great if you could leave a review. It doesn't have to be long only a few words. This really makes a big difference to authors and can also help readers discover new books.

To find out more about my other releases, head to *www.redjackalbooks.co.uk* where, if you subscribe to their mailing list, you'll not only receive up-to-date information on releases, promotions and competitions but also a free gift - free samples of my bestselling thrillers!

I also welcome your feedback, comments and questions. You can get in touch with my via my website or on social media media:

Twitter: @Jmathersauthor
Facebook: https://www.facebook.com/Jmathersauthor
Instagram: @jmathersauthor

About the Author

Joseph Mathers is a former aid worker, teacher and journalist who began his first thriller while working in Egypt. Since then, his award winning best selling colour series has gone on to delight readers across the world. His work has received widespread critical acclaim, with many reviewers and readers likening Joe's work to authors at the very top of the genre, including Lee Child and Vince Flynn.

And you can follow him on twitter and facebook

@Jmathersauthor

https://www.facebook.com/Jmathersauthor

Made in United States
Orlando, FL
26 October 2023

38241945R00152